THE
FALL OF
DOCTOR
ONSLOW

Also by Frances Vernon

Privileged Children
Gentlemen and Players
A Desirable Husband
The Bohemian Girl
The Marquis of Westmarch

THE
FALL OF
DOCTOR
ONSLOW

FRANCES VERNON

ANDRE DEUTSCH

First published in Great Britain in 1994 by
Andre Deutsch Limited
105 Great Russell Street, London WC1B 3LJ

Cataloguing-in-publication data
for this title is available from
the British Library

ISBN 0 233 98875 0

Printed in Great Britain by
WBC Bridgend

Author's Note

Some readers may think that the story told in this novel is wildly improbable. I want to assure them that the central plot of *The Fall of Doctor Onslow* is historical: I lifted it from the story of the dramatic resignation of Dr C. J. Vaughan, Headmaster of Harrow 1844–59, as recounted in the Memoirs of John Addington Symonds. The characters, on the other hand, are fictional, and I am not presenting them as portraits under different names of the people involved in the real affair. Some bear more resemblance than others to their originals, but most are either total invention, or else are made up of a lot of imaginary flesh on an incomplete, historically-suggested skeleton.

Frances Vernon, London,
1991

1

When the young Doctor of Divinity George Robert Onslow was made Headmaster of Charton in 1844, he was put in possession of one of the fattest appointments available to a clergyman. Charton School had such generous endowments that, his residential perquisites aside, the Headmaster could draw from the foundation almost five thousand pounds a year. Boarding-house profits and capitation fees for each pupil ought to have raised the sum still further, but when Dr Onslow arrived, profits and capitation fees amounted to very little, for there were only sixty boys in the school where once there had been three hundred.

Dr Onslow was determined to raise the number of pupils to over four hundred as soon as possible. His motive was not a desire to increase his stipend, but a sense of duty, and an eager desire to reform: Charton's numbers had sunk because the place was notorious for drunkenness, lawlessness, and failures at Oxford and Cambridge. It was one of the very worst public schools in England, and Dr Onslow had been appointed to make it the best.

He did not mean to rescue Charton from its decayed state by entirely overturning the developments of the past two hundred years, ceasing to educate the sons of the rich, and remembering the wishes of the school's founder – who, in Queen Mary's reign, had established a free school for the benefit of local people. Instead, he meant to reform it on the lines laid down by the celebrated Dr Arnold of Rugby, one of whose favourite pupils he had been: he meant to turn out Christian gentlemen, the best of whom would also be scholars.

Dr Onslow was successful in his aims, and by 1858, when he had been Headmaster for fourteen years, his success had taken material shape. All but two of the school buildings were the product of his reign, and these new buildings were the symbol of his moral and academic victory.

═══

The school was situated near London, in the village of Charton Underhill. On the crest of the little hill which gave the village its name there was a railway station, and looking down from the station it was possible to see the brick results of Dr Onslow's work. They fell gently away down a winding road, and the Headmaster was pleased to see that the most noticeable of all was the chapel he had built.

Closest to the station was the steepled parish church, but it was largely hidden from view by a group of elm-trees. Below and to the left, there could be seen the massive house known as Great School, while across the way there was the more convenient Little School, erected by Dr Onslow to house the overflow of boys from the old class-rooms. Further down was the red and grey, pure Gothic chapel, while beyond were various boarding-houses and the Headmaster's own residence, a plain and heavy structure with rectangular windows, where he lived with his wife in one half, while forty boys lived in the other.

The surrounding countryside was pleasant but dull, being flat on the whole, and dominated by isolated trees and hawthorn hedges. It was being gradually encroached upon by the new villas that came inching along the London and North-Western Railway, but in 1858 there were still nearly three miles of open country between Charton Under-hill and the furthermost outskirts of London. Dr Onslow therefore did not consider the wisdom of persuading the trustees to buy up land, and so prevent his school's being swallowed up in the end.

Of all the school buildings, only Great School itself went back to the time of Charton's founder. It was of dark brick, and had been given a fortress-like appearance by its high windows, the lowest row of which was some fifteen feet above the ground. A long flight of steep steps ran up to the main entrance, and the house was surrounded by a yard fenced in with iron railings where, on half-holidays, the boys stood and answered to their names.

Inside Great School there were three classrooms, and the largest and most important of these was known as the Lower Room. Originally, the whole school had been taught here, for there was room for eighty pupils, and it had not at first been intended that Charton should cater for more. It was long and narrow, and beneath the windows that showed nothing but sky there was wooden panelling, black with age, on which the names of countless schoolboys had been deeply carved.

Round the walls there were grouped rows of benches, each arranged in front of a high seat for a master. There were no desks. Such a seating-plan made it impossible for anything but Latin and Greek to be taught, and taught according to the ancient method of getting by heart, reciting aloud, and construing phrase by phrase. Dr Onslow did not think of changing this method; he found it perfectly satisfactory for younger boys at least, and under him the three most junior forms continued to be taught together in the Lower Room.

On a cold February morning in 1858, Dr Onslow came into the Lower Room, took a slippery raised seat usually occupied by one of his colleagues, and began to overawe his younger pupils. He did this twice in each term, six times a year. It used to be only four, but recently he had replaced the two school half-years of tradition with the three terms more appropriate to a railway age; the boys had been glad of this change, but they wished he had decided he need now examine them only once a term.

3

Dr Onslow adjusted the folds of his gown, brushed his cuff, and smiled faintly at the anxious faces below him. Some of the boys were not looking at him, they were hiding their eyes. He glanced swiftly round the room to see that all in this familiar scene was as it should be. Across from him the boys of the other two forms were conning their books in the grey light from the windows, waiting for their turn: he was satisfied, and turned his eyes once more to those in front of him.

The boys were not all of an age. They were placed in school solely according to their academic competence, and so the Shell form contained a large number of fourteen year olds, some bright and diligent children of twelve and thirteen, a few boys in their middle teens, and one young man nearly old enough to shave. They all wore blue coats, but their trousers and waistcoats were not uniform. In spite of this Dr Onslow found it difficult to tell them apart. He paid the minimum of attention to boys below the Sixth, whom he taught in person. Only the intelligent ever reached the Sixth, and except insofar as he was responsible for their morals, he was not interested in those who were not intelligent.

Brains bought power and privilege at Charton. It was not to boys of strong character that Dr Onslow deputed a part of his authority over the juniors, but to those who had succeeded in their lessons, some of whom were no more than fifteen. Dr Arnold had operated the same system, and Dr Onslow, who had been three years under him in the Sixth at Rugby, believed in its surpassing excellence.

'Shall we begin?' he said. Catching the eye of one of the older boys, he went on: 'What is your name?'

'Young, sir.'

'Well Young, you are supposed to have mastered the first few paragraphs of the seventh book of the Aeneid. Repeat them, if you please.'

His choosing an older boy first of all showed that he was not in his best mood. When feeling genial, he liked to give the younger ones a chance to demonstrate their cleverness; when feeling less amiable, he chose the fools well on into adolescence, and abused them with a coolly scornful tongue for their mistakes.

'*Tu quoque litoribus nostris,*' said Young slowly and carefully as he got to his feet, '*Aeneia nutrix, aeternam moriens famam, Caieta, dedisti; et nunc servat honos – sedem tuus, ossaque nomen Hesperia in magna, si qua est ea gloria* – um – um – *signat*.

'*At pius exsequiis Aeneas* – *rite solutis, aggere compasito, composito . . .*'

Onslow sat still as an owl, listening to the hesitations. He did not even drum his fingers on the wooden arm of his chair; that was not his way. Presently he interrupted the boy, and said:

'Very well, now construe.'

Young, who had wound himself up like a musical box, uttered three more words before the sense of Onslow's order penetrated his mind. He paused for a while, breathing deeply, then began again:

'*Tu quoque*, you – thou also, *litoribus nostris*, to our coasts, *Aeneia nutrix*, Aeneas's nurse, *aeternam moriens famam*, eternal fame by death have given . . .' He struggled on for one more sentence, then was stopped. Onslow said softly:

'Your crib must have been a very bad one if it could not do a little more for your construction of an English sentence. At your age you ought to be able not merely to make a literal translation, but to render the Latin in tolerable prose. I need scarcely add that your literal translation ought to be accurate. Shores, not coasts, in the first line! Or perhaps you disagree, and think that is rather a matter of style? I am sure you know best.' Onslow's quiet sarcasms were dreaded by his pupils.

The boy muttered: 'Sir, I didn't use a crib.' He was lying when he said this.

'Naturally I take your word for that,' said Onslow. Dr Arnold had made a point of never doubting a boy's given word, and he did the same. 'I am glad of it, but try in future to think a little harder. Think a few phrases ahead – and now sit down.'

5

He passed on to another boy, making a mental note to repent later of having in effect accused a boy of cribbing without sound evidence. Yet cribbing was so rife in all schools that it was reasonable to assume any randomly chosen boy was guilty – like bullying, it was something far more difficult to stamp out than drunkenness, poaching, and such violent amusements as stoning the townspeople's horses. Onslow had dealt with all those long ago.

'. . . *cum venti posuere omnisque repente resedit flatus et in lento lucantur marmore tonsae atque hic Aeneas ingentem* . . .' recited one of the younger boys, searching for approval with his eyes on Onslow's unmoved face.

Onslow's was a sallow face, oval and calm and not quite handsome. His mouth was small and firm, with a slightly protruding lower lip, and his nose was long and faintly curved. He had grey, well-shaped but rather small eyes, a round chin, and a good head of thick brown hair. Though he was forty-two years old, his face was unlined, and his movements had the grace of confident youth. A flowing gown, and the black and white of his clerical dress, became him well; not because they suited his figure and his colouring, but because they gave him a starkly imposing look. Two things were wrong with his appearance: he was only five foot six, and he had narrow, sloping shoulders. The boys made much of both of his figure's deficiencies and of his yellow complexion.

'Thank you,' Onslow said to the boy who was repeating his lesson.

As he spoke, he noticed activity on the back bench: watching intently, he saw that the boys were using their shuffling feet to pass something along the floor. In a very gentle voice he said:

'Hand that note, or whatever it may be, to me.'

The boy who was treading on it at that moment jumped and blinked at him.

'At once,' said Onslow.

'Yes, sir.' He hurried to pick it up.

The note was handed over. Onslow unfolded it and read words scribbled in a big, clumsy, childish hand.

6

'Darling Lucy,' it said, 'I have a good bed ready so meet me this afternoon after football if you can contrive it. Yours with love.'

Onslow stared at the words for some time, then he laid the note on his lap, and a dark flush crept under his skin.

'I have forbidden the use of female names,' he said clearly. Then: 'Who is the author of this? Who had disobeyed me?'

After a moment's pause the oldest boy in the class got to his feet. He looked a gangling twenty, though he was not quite seventeen.

'You,' said Onslow, as though he meant to say 'the chiefest idiot in the school'. The boy dared to look at him, and saw in Onslow's face not horrified rage and distress, but a mere hint of disgusted irritation. It was rare for Onslow to show any feelings at all. 'For whom was this intended?' said Onslow, whose flush had now drained away, leaving him pale.

'For Cooper, sir.'

'Stand up Cooper.'

A pretty thirteen year old rose from the other end of the back bench, looking terrified.

'You will do five hundred lines. You,' he said to another boy, whose nerves were making him grin shakily, 'will stop smirking, unless you want the same.'

'Yes, sir.'

'Sit down.' He paused. 'You will not meet Cooper this afternoon, Brandon. You will meet me, here, for a very different purpose.' Floggings were always carried out in the Lower Room. 'I will not tolerate disobedience of any kind.'

'Yes, sir – no, sir.'

'I will forgive a great deal,' said Onslow to the whole form, 'but I will not forgive arrogant stupidity. Did you imagine that I would not notice what you were doing there, passing this along? The whole of the back row may do a hundred lines.' He tore the note to Lucy Cooper into shreds, and scattered the shreds on the floor.

Onslow did not realise that his voice, though smooth and level as always, had risen in volume and cut across the

7

room. He failed to notice that it was not only the Shell boys who were staring at him, waiting for worse, but the boys of the Upper and Lower Fourth, whose books lay forgotten in their laps.

2

Onslow flogged Brandon at two o'clock, wiped the incident from his mind, and retired to his study for the rest of the afternoon. It was a Thursday, a half-holiday, and like the boys senior enough not to have to fag for their elders or be kicked by them at football, he was free to spend it as he wished.

After reading some Sixth Form essays on the Athenian constitution, he went to his desk, and there spent a long time in composing a letter to *The Times*. *The Times*, a Radical newspaper, had recently criticised him for allowing the senior boys too much power: there had been a minor scandal a few weeks before, when a young fag was beaten so hard by a monitor that his back had required a doctor's attention.

From his study window, Onslow could see boys passing in the street. Looking up from his letter just before it was time to have the curtains closed, he noticed one of his favourite sixth-formers walking arm in arm with a younger boy, earnestly talking. He smiled to see them. Both were carrying sketch-books, and he guessed that they had been drawing some part of the parish church's architecture, for the sixth-former was fascinated by all things medieval and loved to communicate his interest.

Inspired by the sight of the two boys, Onslow was able to finish his difficult letter to *The Times* on a high, bold note. He turned it into a passionate defence of the old English system of education, in which boys were largely untroubled by masters outside lesson-hours, and kept discipline themselves. This system, he said, favoured the development of a manly character. Responsibility turned boys into men. Freedom enabled them to develop intense, improving friendships, and keen interests of their own which might be of great consequence in later life. Faults committed outside the schoolroom ought therefore to be the province of masters only in exceptional cases. To be sure, there were sometimes unfortunate incidents when older boys enforced discipline, but so there were when masters did. On the whole, the products of a modern public school compared very well with those of schools run on the Continental model, where boys were constantly supervised, like children.

Onslow concluded by pointing out that whereas it used to be the case that masters ignored boys entirely outside school, nowadays the Headmaster attempted to be a Christian guide and friend to his pupils: a friend and pastor, he emphasised, not a policeman. Then he laid down his pen, wondered whether he could be said to live up to his own ideal, and sealed the letter.

━━

That evening after chapel, when Onslow and his wife and brother-in-law were finishing their dinner in a crimson dining-room, the boys of Mr Taylor's house discussed the events of the morning in surroundings of noisy decay.

Taylor's was a typical boarding-house, modern and cheaply built, with rattling windows, mean fireplaces, and leaky gas-brackets. It smelt of latrines, mice and cabbage. Directly inside the boys' entrance there was a rickety staircase, overshadowed by walls coated with arsenic-rich, dark green paint. On each landing there were many doors, for the boys of Charton did not sleep in dormitories and prepare their lessons in classrooms as at many schools, but slept and worked in rooms for two or three at most – some tried to make them homelike, with pictures and ornaments and improvised curtains. From after supper until morning chapel at seven, the boys were supposed to be in their rooms, but sometimes they slipped out. Their master Mr Taylor took little interest in them: he left their discipline

10

largely to his head-of-house, a thin shy Sixth Form boy called Christian Anstey-Ward, who detested him, the house, and the school, and found it hard to discipline anyone.

Christian Anstey-Ward and another sixth-former were helping each other to prepare their next day's lessons when they heard the flimsy door of the next room being roughly pushed open.

'How's your arse, Brandon? Let a fellow see!'

'Hang it, let me alone can't you?'

'He's only sitting on one cushion; can't be so very bad,' said a third voice.

'Come, how many cuts did you get?'

Christian Anstey-Ward got up to poke his little fire, and when he turned back, he saw that his companion was grinning.

'What's so amusing, Bright?' he said pleasantly.

'Oh, don't you know? Brandon was fool enough to try to make an assignation with that pretty little bitch of his from Montague's – he passed a note in school, and of course he was caught. Onslow read it – I'd give a sovereign to know just what the note said.' 'Bitch' was the usual Charton term for the young lover of an older boy.

Christian blinked with interest, but all he could find to say was:

'Onslow?'

'Don't you remember that he was examining the lower forms this morning?'

'Oh, of course. So – so what happened?'

'So Onslow flogged him for it.'

'I still do not understand why it is amusing,' said Christian, sitting down.

'Oh, I promise you, it's mightily amusing.'

'Why so?' said Christian.

Bright lowered his eyes.

'Oh, only because he thinks he's up to snuff, when he is not. How would it be if he knew how many of us play the same game as Brandon?'

11

Christian stared at the book in front of him, and tore at the corner of a page.

'It sounds almost as though he punished Brandon for writing a note in school, not for the note's contents, and for my part I cannot think that right,' he said. 'A flogging of three cuts is what one would get for failing to learn a lesson, or some offence of that kind.'

'How very strict you are,' responded Bright, thinking that this perhaps had something to do with the fact that Christian was plainer than most of the boys at Charton. He had thin sandy hair, a poor complexion, a very wide mouth, and deep-set eyes that seemed to have no lids. 'Since you can't order Brandon's expulsion, why don't you at least put a stop to the unseemly behaviour next door?'

'I will if it does not stop soon.'

There was no unseemly behaviour, but there was a good deal of rowdy talk. One of the boys echoed Bright, saying:

'Suppose he flogged every fellow who has a bitch? Think of his poor arm.'

'Don't forget the bitches too.'

'You'll have to have your precious Lucy spread ointment on your sores tomorrow, Brandon. What a pity he ain't in this house.'

'Ain't it just?' said Brandon, trying to resign himself to being teased. 'Go away, won't you?'

'Not I. I've been a good boy, done all my verses for tomorrow: at least, I don't intend to do any more. Are those macaroons over there? Let me have one, you're too fat as it is, you shouldn't eat them.' The speaker seized the cracked plate and passed it round.

'Very good, most delicious. I'm sure your mama would be pleased to know you bought them for your friends not for yourself, she must be so much worried about your being fat. The thought of you munching them all alone would very likely give her a spasm, you know, Brandon, and you ought to think of that, you know.'

Two other boys giggled sycophantically as they ate the macaroons, and one of them took up the theme, saying thickly:

12

'Not to mention your governor's spasm when he learns about your bill at the pastrycook's. You shouldn't have gone on tick, my boy, not a good idea at all, and damme if I won't ask Onslow to flog you for it.'

'Give them back!' said Brandon against the laughter.

'No, you're well served for being such a muff as to be caught by Onslow. I'll bet we have to endure a damn lowering sort of sermon on Sunday, all about the lustful and Kibroth-Hathaavah, and you know how in general he leaves that sort of thing alone. He'll tell all the monitors to watch us and report to him. And the masters too, I shouldn't wonder.'

'Little does he know the nature of monitors.'

'Or masters?'

They went on attempting to be witty. Next door, neither Bright nor Christian was able to concentrate on work. Bright had no objection to listening through the wall, but Christian, who did object, was temporarily lost in thoughts of the contrast between life in this smelly house and life in his dream-world, which he called 'Hellas'.

Yet the contrast was not absolute, for the conversation in Brandon's room was not wholly unlike certain conversations in 'Hellas'.

'Hellas' was the idea of ancient Greece which Christian had derived from the *Phaedrus* and *Symposium* of Plato. He had watered these works with his own imagination, and built up a vivid picture of a world in which men's pure and spiritual love for each other was a ruling principle. Though 'Hellas' was the historical Greece, about whose civilization Christian meant one day to write books, winter, work and women did not exist there. Corn and wine and olives sprang up effortlessly from the soil, and under the olives, grave philosophers and handsome athletes talked about beauty, truth, the stars, and their love. Their love was passion for the Ideal as it happened to be embodied on earth, thought Christian, after Plato.

'Lejeune and Sillitoe were nearly caught in bed together yesterday,' said one of the boys in Brandon's room.

13

Christian's brief vision of 'Hellas' was over, and he heard this. He looked up angrily, and his eyes met Bright's.

Bright was reckoned to be an attractive youth: he had a good figure, dark wavy hair, neat little features, and slanting eyes of a curiously light, brilliant brown. Christian did not think him handsome, perhaps because he had a prejudice against curly hair dating back to his early childhood, when an older cousin happened to say that in his opinion curly hair was vulgar. He noticed now that Bright also had a nose so far removed from the Grecian that it barely escaped being snub.

'Why can't they for once talk about football, or bird's-nesting, or food?' Christian blurted out. 'Surely to goodness this subject has been sufficiently thrashed out!'

Bright shrugged. 'I don't know, but as far as food is concerned, I've a meat-pie in my room, and some beer. When we have finished you can share it with me if you will.' Bright and Christian were not close friends, but each found the other the least disagreeable person in Taylor's.

'Anything except this filth!'

'It ain't filth, it's only nature. If we had access to – female society, it would not happen.'

'Nature!'

'You happen to prefer art. I'm not sure but what I don't too.' Bright hesitated, and dug his hands deep in his pockets. 'There are one or two things I'd like to tell you, if you really think you know the worst – '

'I'm going to put a stop to it.'

'I have been wondering why you did not do so ages ago, if it disgusts you so.'

Christian went out, threw open the door of Brandon's room, and nearly tripped over a crate containing a hibernating tortoise.

'Go to your own rooms, this has been going on long enough.'

They paused, not daring to defy him openly because he had the power to cane them, and when he was angry he used it. Like Onslow, when he did strike, he struck hard.

'I mean what I say. Go now.'

14

They filed out slowly. Christian, turning, saw that Bright had joined him on the landing.

'Oh, so you were in there were you, Dolly?' he said to a blond boy of fourteen. He had been able to distinguish his bitch's voice quite clearly. 'Go and see to the fire in my room, and then you can clean my boots, they're by my bed. But give me a kiss first.'

Bright shot a quick look at Christian, who blushed deeply, flung himself back into his room, and slammed the door. Bright's little bitch was nearly lovely enough to live in 'Hellas' – but he was neither sufficiently intelligent nor sufficiently pure in heart.

3

The air was crisp but the sky was dull, and tired snow lay in patches under the hedgerows and on the faded pasture. Black tree-tops full of old rooks' nests swept the grey clouds, and down below, early and feeble primroses which had opened in a mild spell lay frozen, not worth the picking. Rotten leaves with a lace edging of frost clogged the sides of the lane, and a multitude of puddles contained squeaking shards of ice.

'What a dreary winter this is, and I suppose we may expect more snowfalls,' said Louisa Onslow to her brother Martin. 'Such horrid weather for the poor Princess Royal's wedding journey. I wonder the Queen did not put it off till the spring.'

They were driving along the lane in a smart gig, and Louisa was handling the reins. Although she complained of the weather, she was an active woman, and did not like to stay indoors all day even when it was cold.

'I wonder too,' said her brother, 'though even a few months' difference would not have made a child out of the nursery old enough to be married.'

'Nonsense!' smiled Louisa, who knew he was teasing her, but took the bait. 'I was scarcely older when I married Dr Onslow.'

Louisa rarely called her husband by his Christian name. She had been married to him for eleven years, but the wifely 'George' was beyond her; to her it seemed in an odd way more solemn and formal than 'Dr Onslow'. Martin Primrose thought it was as though Louisa's early and childless marriage had shut her into perpetual girlhood: she was nearly thirty years old, but she looked more like twenty-four.

She and her brother were very much alike, yet where Louisa was attractive, her brother was remarkably plain. Louisa was not a beauty. Her thick hair was flaxen, not golden as she would have liked, and her face was too pointed at the chin, with very high, wide cheekbones, and a thin narrow nose. Her ears were a great trouble to her, for they were undeniably too large, and stuck out too much – but the prevailing mode of dressing the hair in a smooth bag-like arrangement effectively concealed this. She was also too thin to show rounded shoulders and a hint of round bosom when she wore evening dress, but all these faults were carried off into insignificance by her tiny, pretty mouth, and her remarkable eyes. Her eyes were almost as large as a cat's or a child's, with unusually heavy lids, an upward tilt at the outer corners, and light specks in their grey-green irises which when she was animated could look like bubbles of liveliness.

It was as though a clever modeller had taken her brother Martin's long face and given it tiny, charming twists, taking off the slightly bulbous tip to his nose, reducing the size of the ridiculous ears by an important fraction, enlarging the eyes, thickening the hair, removing the lantern jaw. Onslow, who loved his brother-in-law and old school-friend dearly, thought that the expert modeller had taken away not only Martin's plainness, but also the masculine intelligence of his expression, and the innocence and freshness of a novice's attempt at making a human face.

Martin Primrose was a canon of Maidstone, and he cared nothing for his lack of beauty; not because as a Christian he ought not to, but because he had never found himself in a situation where a handsome face would have been an advantage. He was unmarried, and had never wanted to marry, or do anything but continue to live with his mother, who had kept house for him since she was widowed ten years before. Like Onslow, he was forty-two, but he still felt too young for a wife.

17

'I am so glad you agreed to drive out with me,' said Louisa. 'Dr Onslow does not like me to go alone in a gig, he seems to think it not only dangerous but nearly as improper as going alone in a hansom in London. So the result of it is that I am scarcely ever able to drive. I suppose I might take a groom up beside me, indeed I do when I am on some errand, but it quite spoils the pleasure. Having you is quite another matter.'

'You drive very well,' said Primrose. He paused. 'Louie, I have a feeling there is something on your mind – you are speaking too intently of trivialities. What is it? Do you want to tell me?'

'I must, for it concerns you,' said Louisa, sighing. 'How right you always are!' She turned the gig round an awkward corner, and then told him: 'I am so much afraid that you and Dr Onslow will quarrel, and I couldn't bear it. If we did not see you often I do not think I could – I would be so lonely!' She said no more.

He squeezed her arm: he knew that Onslow did not confide in her as a man ought to in his wife.

'Quarrel? My dear Louie, why should we?'

'About religion. You know how your views differ, and Dr Onslow was so much shocked by that sermon you preached in December, the one about Hell that caused such a storm. Please, please do not mention it to him, and if he mentions it, I beg you to be as conciliating as possible.'

'Of course I won't mention it if you do not wish me to, but I promise you, you have no need to be in a worry. However I may regret George's high-churchmanship, he is my dearest friend, just as he says I am his. We may disagree, but we shan't quarrel seriously – not about anything, Louie.'

'I do not think it is fair to call him a high churchman.'

'My dear, let us only say that he so detests Evangelicals and to some extent Broad Churchmen, he often finds himself in agreement with the more moderate kind of high churchman.'

Primrose himself was an extreme Broad Churchman. He minimised the importance of difficult or unpleasant doc-

18

trines, rejected the substitutionary theory of the Atonement as immoral, regretted all divisions between Protestant Christians, considered that the terms of clerical subscription to the Thirty-Nine Articles ought to be relaxed, and was a keen supporter of State supremacy in religious affairs. He was tolerant of everything except bigotry. Had the bodily resurrection of Christ been proved to be untrue by archaeological researches, Primrose would not have been seriously disturbed, because to his mind the message of Christianity would remain unaffected even by the discovery of Christ's body. As it was, he maintained a discreet silence on the subject of Christ's divinity and resurrection, and this made people suspect him not merely of Latitudinarianism but of Socinianism, of actual disbelief in these two tenets of his faith.

Primrose was a well-known man in the Church of England, a writer and a leader of his party, which was called Broad Church or Arnoldian by its friends, and Latitudinarian by its enemies. He was in the forefront of every movement for liberalisation or reform, not only in the Church but in the universities. A few years before, he had drawn scandalized attention to himself by giving passionate support to Frederick Denison Maurice, a professor at King's College London who had been deprived of his post for stating that Hell, though eternal, could not be everlasting because it was outside time. In December, he had trumped Maurice by preaching and publishing a sermon which most people believed said there was no Hell at all: though in fact, Primrose had said that while Hell was not a lake of fire and brimstone or a place of positive spiritual torment, it was the absence of consciousness, and therefore of the Beatific Vision – it was, literally, eternal death. He had also hinted that no more than a tiny fraction would be condemned even to this mild Hell, and that any other view was incompatible with the doctrine of God's mercy.

Holding such liberal views, he could not hope for the bishopric or deanery which might have been his due had he been more orthodox, but Primrose did not care. He did

19

not care even when people said that it was wrong for him to be a clergyman at all. Onslow was among those who believed this, though neither he nor his wife would have dared to tell him so, for fear of distressing him and losing his friendship.

'I confess,' Primrose said now, 'that I wish George had found it possible to hold by Dr Arnold's churchmanship as he has held by his schoolmastership, if there is such a word.'

'He must wish it were possible too, or so I imagine, for he has never said so directly. He always says Dr Arnold was a father to him.'

'He does not talk about such things to you very often, does he?'

'No.'

Onslow knew that Louisa, like her brother and her parents, was a Latitudinarian – but she never attempted to argue with him, and he passed the matter over in silence.

'Oh dear,' said Louisa suddenly, looking along the road. An open carriage was bowling towards them. 'I am sure that's Mrs Salcombe – I expect she is trying to play the great lady, visiting cottagers. I wonder whether they are grateful?' She added: 'I shall have to cut her. She left cards on me the other day, and I never returned, but she did not take the hint – when I happened to see her in the street she tried to treat me as an old acquaintance. It is so hard to know what to do when people will not abide by society's rules. Here she comes.'

Louisa drove on, looking straight ahead, and Primrose, raising his hat a fraction, noticed Mrs Salcombe waggling her hand. The cut was accomplished, Louisa said.

'There! it makes me feel unkind, but I cannot endure the thought of having to recognise someone whom I thought both ill-bred and dull when she was introduced to me. Am I right in thinking Dr Onslow wishes he were still true to Dr Arnold's notions, Martin?'

'Oh, yes,' said Primrose. 'We have discussed it – not quarrelled, Louie, discussed. As I say, he regrets it, but he maintains that of all the world, only Dr Arnold was capable

20

of remaining a good man while holding lax views on doctrine.'

'Hm!' said Louisa. 'I am very sure he added that you too are so capable.'

Primrose said nothing to this, because Louisa was right. He sighed, and went on: 'He insists that for everyone else sound doctrine alone is the protector of morals, which, you must own, is a High Church position. But to go back to your worry, Louie, I can only promise you that if there was no lasting breach between us when George truly *was* a high churchman, there will not be one now.'

'When was that?' said Louisa with interest.

'My dear, did he never tell you? He was once not merely high, but a full-blown Tractarian. Remember we were at the university when the Tracts were just coming out. He was entirely seduced for quite a year?'

She was so startled that she dropped the reins.

'Directly after you had left Rugby! I cannot believe it, when Dr Arnold was still alive – and you were not even at Oxford, you were at Cambridge!' Cambridge had been largely unaffected by the exciting demands which poured out from Oxford in the series of pamphlets called *Tracts for the Times* – demands for a dedicated Catholic priesthood with spiritual powers far above those of the laity, for the revival of fasting and confession, for clerical supremacy in church affairs, and for an attitude of deep mystical reverence towards the Sacrament. Unlike ordinary high churchmen, who merely stuck close to the doctrines and traditions of the Church of England and hated dissenters, the Tractarians cherished a medieval vision of the Church set against the World, of a ship afloat on a black sea, outside which there could be no salvation.

Primrose laughed at Louisa's amazement.

'Certainly George never dared mention it to Dr Arnold, though I believe he reproached himself for not seeking a martyr's crown in doing so. I ought not to laugh – the poor fellow suffered considerably, torn between his new convictions and his old loyalties.'

'Did he fast?' said Louisa. 'Did he have minute struggles

with his conscience over whether or not he could celebrate a saint's day by eating a second piece of bread and butter? Did he rail against Protestantism, like Mr Hurrell Froude?'

'Well, I do not think he went quite so far as to echo Froude in condemning Latimer and Ridley to the stake a second time, but I promise you, it was all most distressing.'

'Good gracious! I should think it must have been!' Though she said this, Louisa was smiling at the picture in her mind's eye of her husband being so childish.

'I think the problem was that George's temperament is somewhat melancholy, he is sadly apt to lose faith in human nature,' said Primrose. 'I know it seemed to him in those days that our national faith was in so much danger we could only save it by retreating into ecclesiasticism, ignoring all progress, thundering anathemas. The perfect opposite of all Dr Arnold had taught us.'

He hesitated, and Louisa looked inquiringly at him, knowing there was more.

'I do not know,' he said, 'but I fancy – I fancy that removed from the Doctor's immediate influence, he may have come close to losing his faith altogether. It must have shocked him most dreadfully, it was not something he could ever have expected, and he rushed into the arms of Newman in an attempt to save himself – buried himself in ritual and mortifications, took to himself all their notions of the possibility of losing baptismal grace. He must have thought that had happened to him. Remember how very full of wickedly despairing ideas about the unwisdom of trusting to God's love and mercy Newman was – I suspect it would all have seemed very plausible to George, if he felt himself suddenly gripped by doubts. Then when he became sure of his faith again – if I am right – he grew more moderate, and of course, since Newman went over to Rome he has regarded all Ritualists with suspicion.'

'Do you think he ever thought of going over to Rome himself?' said Louisa.

'Oh no. Remember this phase of his fortunately did not last for long – less than two years, he never had time to wonder about that.'

'I wish he had told me about this.'

'I daresay he has forgotten, or he is ashamed.'

Louisa said, a little fretfully:

'I can only think all these divisions and distinctions are the height of folly, and unchristian, too. We ought all to tolerate each other.'

'An admirable sentiment, Louie, but you must remember things are a little more complicated in real life. Remember how much harm the high churchmen do, with their refusal to compromise over subscription. They won't allow us to be tolerant, and neither in their own way will the Evangelicals – you know you've said so yourself.'

'Like Dr Onslow,' said Louisa, 'now that he is so secure in his faith that he cannot perceive why anyone else should be less so.'

Primrose sighed.

They were silent for a while, and Louisa turned the gig back towards Charton. After a few minutes' trotting, she turned to her brother and said cheerfully:

'Well, whatever else, you and I and Dr Onslow find ourselves in agreement when it comes to the odiousness of Evangelicals. I must take what comfort I can from that.'

'Very true!' said Primrose. 'I promise to confine my conversation on religious matters to abusing them in the most unchristian way imaginable.'

Louisa smiled, and slapped the reins down on the horse's back, making him break into a canter.

4

Winter sunlight cut like ice through the high and glittering windows, firing the red and blue glass in the chancel to painful intensities of colour. It bleached the faces of the boys who sat rank upon rank in their shallow pews, four hundred and sixty of them all in black and white, and showed up the grey at the back of their necks. The shadows cast by pillars were not dim and peaceful, but divided the space like knives, and between them on the south wall, colder than snow, there stood out the new marble tablet inscribed with names of Charton boys killed in the Crimea.

The sound of the organ died away. Onslow mounted the steps of the pulpit, and waited for total silence to descend, his eyes daring the boys to fidget and cough. The pulpit concealed his lack of physical stature, and he leant forward, and said:

'My text is taken from the Book of Ecclesiastes, chapter four, verses nine and ten: "Two are better than one . . . for, if they fall, the one will lift up his fellow: but woe to him that is alone when he falleth".'

Christian Anstey-Ward perceived no merit in what he saw as the unpleasantly earthbound melancholy of Ecclesiastes, Onslow's favourite book of the Old Testament.

Before he discovered Plato and 'Hellas', Christian had passed through an intensely religious phase, during which he had fed his inchoate longings for a spiritual home with medievalism and Gothic art, and with memories of all Onslow had told him in confirmation classes about the sublime beauty of doctrine. Not until after 'Hellas' came to occupy his mind did Christian acknowledge to himself that he was in fact repelled by much of what conventional religion had to offer: the impossibilities and immoralities of the Old Testament, the barbarian imagery of Heaven's promise in Revelation, the cold dogmatism of St Paul. Yet having acknowledged this, he continued to believe that the more amiable parts of the New Testament were compatible with the *Symposium*, and though his interest in the Gothic faded, and his flirtation with extreme High Churchmanship came to an end, at seventeen he still considered himself to be a Christian of a kind. He was only just beginning to blame Christianity for his masters' inability to see anything but grammar in the works of Greek literature they professed to understand: he imagined Onslow thought it theologically unsafe to see the world as he did, in the light of Platonic truth, and this gave him a thrill of daring.

Onslow preached an impeccably orthodox sermon on his chosen text, though he secretly admired Ecclesiastes for its unchristian stoicism, the permission it gave to retire from the struggle for endless improvement and contemplate reality in stony acceptance. He was a good preacher, whose sermons had been published and compared to Dr Arnold's, and Christian thought those parts of his discourse he heard when his mind was not wandering were admirable, after their fashion. But he found it hard to concentrate, partly because this was the third service and second sermon of the day. Arthur Bright, who was sitting next to him, was finding it equally difficult.

Ten days had passed since Bright had kissed his lover in front of Christian. Since then, Christian had ignored him, and Bright was not indifferent to this. It was the attention of others which served to stave off the loneliness that threatened him like a fog in all his waking hours: even the attention of someone he did not greatly care for was worth having, especially when that person lived in Taylor's. Looking now at Christian's profile, Bright remembered how they used to share an interest in church architecture, and how Christian had become bored with it. He wondered that anyone so plain and so dull should dare to think ill of him and his interests, should prefer loneliness to his company – without sufficient cause.

Onslow had begun his sermon by giving a description of true friendship and the help it afforded in the struggle to attain godliness; he had now moved on to describe counterfeited friendships, which he said were all too common in Public Schools.

'The commonest counterfeit of friendship,' he said, 'is that sort of connection which one of you forms with another by the accident of being inmates of the same house or room, of having the same master or tutor, or by some more entire accident still, which has thrown you together whether you would or no, and out of which has sprung something which either deserves or assumes the name of a friendship. How many of these intimacies, think you, deserve that name, and how many are counterfeits of friendship? Are you and your friend any help to one another? any help, that is, in matters in which it is any advantage to help one another? any help in doing your duty, in resisting your temptations, in advancing towards the goal of life; the near goal, a useful manhood, the further goal, a happy eternity? Again, have you and your friend a common object? Do you even know anything about one another's objects? Are not matters of the highest moment entirely suppressed between you?'

Out of his pocket Bright took a receipted bill and a pencil-stub. Pressing down on his Bible, he scribbled:

'Do you remember once telling me that you suspected Onslow of being something of a hypocrite? You were perfectly right, but you didn't know the half of it. I am tempted by the sermon to reveal to you the Shocking Truth: I have been his bitch for the past 6 months. Do you think this is a counterfeited friendship, or not? I long to know.' This he laid in the gap between Christian's thighs: his eyes were sparkling, his cheeks flushed, his lips twitching, and his heart beating fast.

For two minutes he watched the other read it, and he calmed down rapidly as he did so. At length Christian held out his right hand for the pencil, looking up at Onslow as

26

he did so, not down at the note or at Bright's anxious face. Without lowering his eyes, he wrote:

'Do you expect me to believe you?' at the bottom of the paper. Then, as Bright laid a finger on it, he clamped it down on his leg and added in a scrawl: 'What a very disgusting lie.'

Bright made a sound as he read this. Christian, with a face as motionless as Onslow's when listening to a bad lesson, quickly folded up the note and pushed it deep down into his right trouser-pocket, from where Bright could not extract it without a struggle. No struggle was possible in chapel.

The sermon came to an end, and Onslow left the pulpit. During the remainder of the service, Christian did not once look in Bright's direction, and when it was over and they were at last able to leave, he flung away from him and walked swiftly off alone, up towards the open country behind the parish church. After half a mile, he came to a five-barred gate, set back a little from the road, and climbed over. Hidden behind the hedge there was an old tree-stump, which he had discovered his first term at Charton, and on this he went to sit down. The countryside round about offered nothing better in the way of a private place.

Seated at last, Christian blinked miserably at the orange and gold of the westering sun, gleaming out from under a cold eiderdown of cloud. His flesh soon became chilled, for his clothes were inadequate and the tree-stump was icy, but he did not consider going back yet. He had come here to think. It was hard to think. When he tried to do so, he only realised that his reaction to Bright's note had not been that of someone who honestly believed what it said to be a stupid lie intended to shock him; and this distressed him, for it meant he would be laughed at. The thought of gross laughter at his expense was unbearable, almost worse than the thought that Bright had not lied.

Possessed of the knowledge that whether Bright's allegation were true or false, the last straw had been laid on his back, all Christian could do for the present was think how much he detested Onslow's school, where such things could happen – especially did he detest its everlasting, dreary religion. Suddenly he resented that religion with extreme bitterness. He remembered Onslow preaching in the pulpit less than an hour ago, preaching calmly, gracefully, as he did every Sunday. Always he preached not on doctrine, but on morals. He reserved the delicate consideration of doctrine for his confirmation classes.

Blowing on his hands to warm them, Christian suddenly remembered how on the night after Brandon was caught making an assignation in school, Bright had dropped certain hints about Onslow's reaction being exceedingly amusing in the circumstances. He remembered his saying that if he indeed thought he knew the worst of Charton . . . His mind now cleared a little, Christian tried to force himself to consider rationally whether Bright had been telling the truth. It was still hard to do so directly, but he remembered Onslow's once placing a hand on his knee when he was reading an essay to him on the sofa in his study. He blushed vividly. At the time he had thought nothing of it, had thought it a mere friendly gesture of warmth and encouragement – a hand on the upper thigh might have been differently interpreted. As it was, it had been agreeable to learn that Onslow was not altogether cold, was more like other men than he seemed. Gestures of physical affection were normal, admirable – sometimes Hellenic.

He is a pasha in a harem of boys, thought Christian now, forgetting that Bright had alleged only that Onslow was engaged in a love-affair with him. The vision of Headmaster Onslow luxuriating in vice like a second Tartuffe was too fascinating to be thrust away, for it would provide a complete explanation of Charton's loathesomeness – but Christian was attempting to be sensible, and after a short while he concluded that the vision could not possibly resemble reality, in spite of that hand on his knee. He could only be thankful that he had called Bright a liar, that if his actions had conveyed doubt, his words had not, and therefore he could not be mocked.

Slowly he got up from his tree-stump, and made his way back to school in the dismal twilight.

5

Though for the boys at Charton most of Sunday was filled with religious services, Onslow was not a devout sabbatarian, and saw no gross immorality in reading secular works or even fiction once church was over. That evening in the drawing room, after dinner and prayers, he said:

'Well, Martin, I finished *Tom Brown's Schooldays* this afternoon.'

Tom Brown's Schooldays had been published the year before, and was enjoying a great success, but it had not come Onslow's way till Primrose gave him a copy, insisting that he read it in spite of his contempt for novels. It was the fact that the book concerned Dr Arnold's Rugby which made Primrose so determined.

'Do you think it gives a fair portrait of Rugby?' said Primrose. 'I cannot think so – I remember nothing whatever of such shocking violence as he describes.'

'My dear Martin, of course it is not a fair portrait of Rugby. It is almost a disgrace.'

'I certainly fail to see why it was necessary to write such lurid and untruthful descriptions of bullying, and fights. The monster Flashman, and so forth. I suppose a certain class of reader is attracted to them.'

'Oh, that! No, the truth is that you were held in such awe you were left in peace, and you were so much preoccupied by higher matters that you noticed nothing that was sordid. I am thinking of the shameful misrepresentation of Dr Arnold.'

'I liked the description of his preaching, the chapel,' said Primrose. 'Did you not, Louie?'

29

'Yes, though naturally I do not know how truthful it is,' said Louisa.

'That was all very well, I grant you, but how can you tolerate Mr Hughes's implying that our master's conception of a manly character resembled Tom Brown? You told me he was at Rugby himself; how could he have come to think that he – Arnold – revered an honest blockhead?'

'He certainly thought it more important to be a Christian than to be a scholar.'

'Certainly! But do you think he would have considered Tom Brown a Christian? Where is his awareness of his Saviour, his awareness of sin? He cares less for Christ than for cricket. And yet Mr Hughes declares at the end of the book that the Doctor was satisfied with him.'

Onslow got up to poke the fire, and Louisa raised her head to look at him. It seemed to her that he was being unduly vehement, and she glanced across at her brother. Meditatively she sucked the end of a piece of silk before using it to thread her needle; this was a habit of which none of her governesses had succeeded in breaking her.

'A manly character,' said Onslow briskly to the fire, 'is not one possessed of what I believe is called a punishing right, or left – do you remember Mr Hughes's remarkable paean in favour of fisticuffs? – but one who is aware of the need to combat sin in himself and in others. Is there one hint in that book that this was our master's view?' It was rare for Onslow to talk in this firmly moral strain outside the pulpit. 'Instead he is portrayed almost as believing that most schoolboy crimes are mere pieces of mischief, scarcely deserving the name of sin. How well I remember his teaching me otherwise.'

'So do I, indeed,' said Primrose.

Onslow turned to him, and said almost angrily:

'My dear Martin, you were as innocent as a newborn kitten, you have never understood sin because you are incapable of committing it and you always were. Do not attempt to make me believe that Arnold ever found it necessary to show you the heinousness of your offences, for you committed none.'

'What nonsense!' Primrose said, though it was true that Dr Arnold had never once found it necessary to correct him. 'Really, I am quite insulted to learn you think that I, in my profession, have no understanding of sin.'

'Your goodness sprang from the heart, as everyone could see,' Onslow went on regardless. He seemed about to say something else, but Louisa interrupted.

'Were *you* ever naughty?'

'Yes,' said Onslow. 'Yes, I was what you choose to call naughty. That was before I knew you, Martin – I was in the Fifth and you were already in the Sixth.'

'What did you do?' said Primrose, looking interested.

'Oh, let us say I broke most of the rules devised for our social and spiritual benefit,' said Onslow. 'But I was never detected, possibly because whatever I did outside school, I was always careful not to neglect my schoolwork. Surely I have told you this before?'

'And I suppose you must have been very careful in other ways,' said Louisa.

'Yes, Louisa, highly skilled in the art of deceit.'

'If you were never detected,' said Primrose, making a steeple of his fingers and raising them to his lips, 'how and why did Arnold show you the error of your ways?'

There was a long pause. Then Onslow replied:

'I entered the Sixth. Is that not a sufficient explanation – that I was thereafter constantly exposed to his mind and his eye?' Having said this, he left his place by the fireplace, went to sit down again, and continued: 'But knowing what I do of parents, I cannot be surprised that the book has been so successful. What a comfort it must be to them to think that the more loutish are their sons, the more they are possessed of Mr Hughes's new cardinal virtue of Englishness.'

Louisa and Primrose both smiled, and the subject was changed.

The same evening, Christian found a letter from Bright waiting for him on the table in his room. It was in a sealed envelope, and when he opened it he read:

My dear Anstey-Ward,
    I give you my word that what I told you in chapel is true, and I take it very hard that you refuse to believe me, only on the grounds, as I suppose, that what I wrote is shocking to your sensibilities.
    It may seem improbable in your eyes, but Onslow is passionately in love with me, and if you will not believe me, I can show you all his letters. In the meantime, as I suppose you will doubt that I do in fact have such letters and will merely think I am lying, I enclose an extract from the latest.
A. J. Bright.

There were words in Onslow's very small and neat but distinctive writing on the enclosed piece of paper, which had been cut off from the bottom of a letter. Trembling now, Christian read:

Beloved boy, it is become an agony to me to see you among your fellows, so keen is my delight in your beauty, so passionate is my wish to separate you from them, to have you alone upon the sofa where we have enjoyed so many, all too brief, moments of love. Can you indeed not come to me on Saturday? Of your loving mercy I ask it.
    Dear Arthur, I beg of you, do not avoid me – I have no time to write more now. I remain, yours through eternity,
    G. R. Onslow.

Christian stared at this for a long time. At length he lowered his candle, put Bright's letter and the signed extract back on the table, and sat down slowly and carefully, caressing his beardless chin all the while like an old man.

After giving his opinion of Mr Hughes's novel, Onslow had retired to his study, saying to Primrose and Louisa that he had letters to write: he sat now on the sofa, thinking about sin.

Onslow's study was a low, dark room, hung with green paper, lined with books, and floored with a thick Turkey carpet. It was precious to him because he liked its enclosed quality, which none of the other rooms in the house shared. When alone there he felt safe, shut away from the world, in control of his surroundings and his emotions – yet it was there that on many occasions he had given free rein to his most dangerous emotions, both in the flesh and on paper.

At present, it was not Arthur Bright who was first in Onslow's thoughts, but Thomas Arnold. By force of contrast, the false portrait of Arnold in *Tom Brown's Schooldays* had aroused half-forgotten memories of the real man, including one particularly painful memory which Onslow believed he would have confided to his brother-in-law had his wife not been present. He knew that his comments upstairs on the novel's inadequacies had been not so much scathing, as he meant them to be, as anguished; and this embarrassed him. Now, pinch-lipped, he could imagine himself telling Primrose just how and why Dr Arnold had shown him the error of his ways, could imagine himself receiving holy understanding – but then he saw himself confessing exactly how, as a man, he had betrayed Arnold's trust in him. Onslow did not think that Primrose would necessarily recoil in horror if he mentioned Arthur Bright. It was conceivable that he would forgive this sin which he could not imagine: but Onslow wanted understanding, not bewildered, sorrowing acceptance, and a plea for him to abandon his evil ways.

The painful image which Onslow dreamt of unloading onto Primrose was a long-suppressed memory which ought to have been wholly pleasurable – the memory of himself aged fifteen, crying and crying with Arnold's hand on his shoulder, weeping with relief at the easing of a vast mental burden.

Onslow remembered how he had approached Arnold

33

with sickly trepidation, driven by a conscience he had not known he possessed. He had been still in the Fifth Form, still deeply afraid of 'Black Arnold', as the man was known to most of his pupils, and had waited in agony for the periodic signal that Arnold was at home to boys who wished to consult him on a personal matter – the hoisting of a flag above the School-house. He went to him expecting to be flogged and expelled; Arnold's kindly smile at his entrance made him blurt out that he deserved both these things.

The truth did not emerge from Onslow's tangled and shivering euphemisms for some time. It was that he and another boy, whom he did not name, had indulged in mutual masturbation in Onslow's minute cubicle of a study. When Dr Arnold learnt this, he was relieved. He had begun to suspect that this most promising of his Fifth Formers was guilty of what he considered the worst of all sins: lying. The sight of Onslow shaking with pain and distress over a moral failing which he regarded as comparatively slight therefore moved him deeply, and so he put a hand on his shoulder, and spoke words of gentle reassurance.

Such a thing had never happened to Onslow before, and it made him burst into passionate tears, an orgy of grief which gradually eased off into the soft weeping of one comforted. Then Arnold began to speak to him about the need to resist temptation, the need both for Christ and for good friends who would assist in the struggle against something which, though minor, could be perilous. Listening to this, sucking in Christian words with new understanding, Onslow thought of how badly he had behaved for months, without ever being caught; and to this new kind father so unlike his own he confessed how he had gone poaching, and drinking, and had broken bounds countless times. He swore that if Arnold would only allow him to remain at Rugby he would never do wrong again. Dr Arnold willingly accepted his assurance, and when Onslow was at last calm enough to leave, he said:

'My dear boy, it is a great pleasure to me to think that I shall have you in the Sixth very soon. Abide by the resolutions you have made today, put your trust in God,

34

and you will become an ornament to the school in the near future, and to the world when you are a man.'

Thereafter, throughout his years in the Sixth Form, Onslow had been treated by Arnold with grave tenderness. He was loved even more than Primrose, because he was a returned prodigal and had had to battle with a difficult nature. Dr Arnold was stern, he often rebuked Onslow for a slight tendency to levity and for intellectual arrogance, but the love he gave him was real, and Onslow struggled to amass more and more of it. With the vast incentive of respect and affection from both Arnold and Primrose, he had found it easy to direct his energies away from every kind of wrongdoing which had tempted him before. He learnt to love Christ, and he never masturbated with another boy again. Those had been the happiest years of his life.

Onslow got up, walked over to his desk, and stood there looking blankly at the text of that day's sermon. Fingering it, he tried to remember exactly why, at fifteen, his conscience had been so very active when the other boy's had not. Then, from deep down inside him, there rose up the memory of his mother discovering him with his hands on his penis when he was six years old. She had beaten him more severely than he had ever been beaten since, and told him that he would certainly go to Hell, a place which she described in great detail, making him scream. Thereafter, till adolescence with its unbearable urges came upon him, he had been too frightened of his own genitals even to look at them. Now Onslow covered his face with his hands, realising that nine years after that incident, he had expected Dr Arnold to behave like his mother. His mother had been a rigid Evangelical, with a fierce hatred of sexuality which was the result of her having suffered a long series of painful miscarriages: but Dr Arnold had been a happily married Latitudinarian, and had taken the official Christian view that lust was the least of the seven deadly sins.

Few who considered themselves truly pious took that official view, which Onslow began to think had corrupted him. He knew now that for years, he had secretly allowed

35

himself to believe that Dr Arnold had sanctioned his little pleasures – it had taken *Tom Brown's Schooldays* to jerk him back into reality. He wondered whether he would have succumbed to temptation in manhood if Dr Arnold had, after all, behaved like his mother – perhaps his sin could have been beaten out of him, even though beating so seldom eradicated sin in the boys at Charton. Perhaps terror would have been effective. But now, he thought, because he had not been doubly terrorised in youth, he could not wholly believe that his keening lust was so very wrong; and thus he went on, from day to day and month to month, loving Arthur Bright without return.

6

'Dr Onslow,' said Louisa next day at luncheon, when Primrose happened to be out, 'I want you to resolve a small difficulty for me. It is very small.'

'Certainly, my dear, if I can.'

'I have spent all morning in trying to decide what to wear to the Taits this evening. It is a choice between pearl grey and pale yellow – which shall it be?'

'But I know nothing of such matters,' said Onslow, picking up his knife and fork again.

'You can surely decide between two colours. I am not asking you to look at the dresses.'

Louisa's two hobbies were her clothes and her garden. When gardening, she wore an old stuff dress with its skirts looped up over a short petticoat, but at all other times her clothes were extremely fashionable and elegant: too much so for a clergyman's wife, Onslow sometimes thought, but he never bothered to speak seriously to her about it.

Onslow's mind was now occupied with Arthur Bright, who had been provocatively idle in school that morning. He said:

'I am very sure it is immaterial which you wear, Louisa. I advise you to spin a coin, if your maid's opinion will not do.'

'But I am asking you,' said Louisa. 'Can you not give me a simple answer?'

'Not when I am not qualified to answer.'

'You are perfectly well qualified to say grey or yellow. That is all I am asking.'

37

They looked at each other across the table. Onslow said in a worried voice:

'My dear Louisa, I see that something is amiss. You are not at all yourself.'

'I am perfectly well. I only want an answer instead of a dismissal of my concerns.'

Onslow paused for a moment.

'I think this particular concern of yours is of little moment and no business of mine, but since you are so determined to extract my opinion, I will say grey. There, are you happy now?'

'Thank you!' said Louisa. 'Thank you for paying me such distinguishing attention.'

In general, Louisa was the most cheerful and least demanding of wives, and Onslow loved her nearly as much as her brother did.

===

The Onslows and Primrose were to dine at Fulham Palace with Dr Tait, the Bishop of London. Dr Tait was an old friend of Primrose's, and they had worked together on the commission which advocated reform of Oxford University some years before; but Onslow did not know the Bishop quite so well, though he too had been a member of the commission.

Both Onslow and Louisa wished to keep Dr Tait's good opinion, because although as Headmaster of Charton Onslow was not subject to his authority, the Bishop of London might prove useful when the time came for him to resign his post. Advancement to a bishopric or deanery was virtually automatic for the retiring headmaster of a great public school, but Onslow's dread was that if prelates and politicians thought little of him, he would be fobbed off with the deanery, and would then be forced to accept a drastic cut in income from nearly six thousand a year to less than a fifth of that – not for a year or two's waiting, but for good. It was for the Prime Minister to decide what should become of him, but the Prime Minister might be influenced by the opinion of senior bishops, especially those appointed by himself. Lord Palmerston, who had appointed Dr Tait, had just resigned from office, but Onslow did not think the new Conservative ministry would last long, and thus he thought it as well to conceal his High Church leanings from Dr Tait in so far as he could do so without hypocrisy, while Louisa sought to appear wise, discreet and serious, without being dowdy. It was to this end she had asked Onslow to choose between two of her more sober evening dresses.

Though quiet in colour and trimmed only with a single fall of lace from the shoulders, Louisa's grey dress was as fashionable as all her others. Its cage crinoline was so large that when they set out to drive to Fulham it took her, her maid and Primrose several minutes to ease it into the carriage, and when at last she was inserted, there was barely room for the two men, though neither of them was large. This gave her an obscure pleasure. Onslow, who had seen Arthur Bright alone that afternoon, made no comment on his wife's taking up so much space, but merely squeezed her hand and complimented her on her looks. Primrose saw the hand-squeeze and wondered very much at the way Onslow sometimes behaved as though he were still courting his wife, when in general he appeared to have no more than an indifferent sort of fondness for her. He said:

'I am being crushed by your skirt, Louie. There is a great steel bar digging into my knee.'

'What you mean,' said Louie, 'is that my skirt is being crushed by you.'

═══

Fourteen people sat round the yellow-lit dinner-table, and Onslow thought he was the worst off of all the guests, certainly worse off than his wife and brother-in-law. Louisa was sitting between her host and a fashionable young man of the type known as a swell, while Primrose had a sensible-looking spinster on one side and a pretty young lady on the other. On Onslow's left there sat Mrs Tait, whom he did

39

not dislike, but on his right there was the elderly and double-chinned wife of a judge, whose idea of conversation was to ask him his opinion on various controversial religious matters, and nod or purse her lips at his replies. She made him feel like a candidate for ordination.

She had already asked him what he thought of Sunday travel, of confession, and of religious sisterhoods – she was inclined to condemn all three, while Onslow was more prone to condemn those who agreed with her, who were nearly always Evangelicals, like his mother. Yet he thought it unwise to express himself as strongly as he might have done, for Dr and Mrs Tait were sympathetic to the more moderate kind of Evangelical. Now, as the entrees were brought in, the judge's lady asked for his opinion of geology and geologists, and of those who admired Strauss's *Life of Jesus*.

'Pray tell me Dr Onslow, which do you think presents the graver danger to faith – geology or neology?'

'Neology, madam,' he said briefly.

'How very interesting. May I ask why so?'

'How very interested you are in my opinions. I must be flattered.' The boys of Charton would have recognised his tone as sarcastic, but the lady inclined her head and said:

'Certainly I am. I am always anxious to discover what clergymen think upon serious subjects. I am surprised, however, that you consider neology the greater threat, for the foolish essays of these German professors are more easily dismissed than the discoveries of science,' she asserted.

'I do not deny that, Mrs Reynolds, though I have no reverence for science. I mean only that once a man has decided that Our Lord worked no miracles, or even that the Book of Daniel is later than the prophet Daniel, in no time at all he is an atheist – though to be sure he may not call himself an atheist. It seems not to be the case that men end similarly who, like myself indeed, come to accept let us say the proposition that the Flood did not cover the whole earth. You must notice that like a scientist, I judge from observation. I own that the geologists have cast doubt

40

on the literal accuracy of the first chapters of Genesis, but the rest of our faith they have left untouched.'

'I do not think I agree with you, Dr Onslow.'

'Do you not, madam?'

'I am persuaded that geology presents a greater danger than you appear to believe. The Book of Genesis is as much a sacred text as the Gospels, and if it must be questioned, that is but the first step towards universal infidelity.'

Onslow said coldly: 'A shocking prospect, madam, and possibly you are right. I will observe only that the Church has survived the assaults of scientists before – how many lost their faith when at last we were obliged to accept that the world is not flat, and that the sun does not go round the earth? A mere handful of men already disaffected.'

'Perhaps you speak justly, Dr Onslow, but I am not sure that I agree.'

'But you believe in a round earth and a heliocentric universe, and remain a Christian, madam, even though both acknowledged facts are contrary to traditional Christian wisdom.'

'Certainly I am a Christian!'

'Our beliefs about the world are incidentals,' said Onslow, forgetting he was talking at a dinner-party to a woman he disliked, 'incidental to the core of our faith in Christ. Greater knowledge of God's design can never shake our faith in Him. No, madam, I fear a man who doubts the morality of the Old Testament or the reality of eternal punishment infinitely more than I fear any scientist.' As he said this, he glanced at Primrose, and bit his lip. As firmly as he disbelieved in Hell, Primrose believed everything the geologists told him, and the less compatible their views were with traditional Christian beliefs the more he liked them. He was not one to prefer the catastrophist theory to the uniformitarian because, distorted a little, it seemed rather more compatible with Genesis.

'You said that you take the gravest view of a man who doubts that Our Lord worked miracles. You forget that geologists, scientists, are more prone irreligiously to doubt miracles than other men,' said Mrs Reynolds.

41

Onslow thought of the great clerical geologist Dr Buckland, who had put his tongue to the liquefying martyr's blood on the floor of an Italian church, and identified it as bat urine. He smiled, and merely said:

'Certain miracles, madam.'

Mrs Reynolds suddenly changed the conversation.

'I am very glad to have had this little talk upon so many subjects with you, Dr Onslow, for a particular reason. Mr Reynolds and I are considering consigning our grandson to your care.'

'Indeed, madam?'

'Therefore I wished to assure myself that your views on serious subjects are broadly in accordance with our own. They are, I find, sufficiently so.'

'I am obliged to you, though you surprise me.'

'But one thing more remains for me to ask. Dr Onslow, the reputation of Charton is excellent, but upon one point I am not yet satisfied — I wish to know how carefully you think it proper to enquire into your prospective pupils' social antecedents.'

Onslow looked her in the eye, and said:

'Dear madam, so long as your grandson behaves himself and his fees are paid, no questions will be asked about his social antecedents.'

The expression on Onslow's face was not malicious, but bland with a hint of solicitude. It took Mrs Reynolds a few seconds to understand his meaning, and when she had understood she wondered in horrified amazement at those who spoke of Dr Onslow as a likely future Archbishop of Canterbury. It was more because of his high reputation than because of her grandson that she had cross-examined him for half an hour, and she now looked forward to telling all who would listen that he was unfit to have charge of a few schoolboys, let alone to sit in Lambeth Palace.

Onslow did not care that he had lost a prospective pupil: Charton was as full as it could hold.

At the other end of the table, Louisa was talking to the fashionable young man on her right, who seemed very much out of place at an episcopal dinner table, but who was related to Dr Tait. They were discussing the question of whether it was possible or prudent to marry on £300 a year, which had recently been receiving attention in the press.

'Would you not find it delightful, Mr Newsome? A little cottage at Brompton, and children round your knee, and fetching your linen home from the washerwoman? So agreeable a change after your nasty club, and curacao, and cigars!'

'Ha! Deuced if I see it myself,' said Mr Newsome, stroking one of his long whiskers as he leant towards her.

'Come, come, don't be so worldly. I am sure you will shock Dr Tait – has he overheard? No, you are safe.'

At that moment, the Bishop turned round and looked kindly at her. He was a big, curly-haired man, handsome in a rather cold and too regular way.

'Mr Newsome and I were discussing the Frugal Marriage question, my lord,' said Louisa. 'Do you think it steadies a young man's character to marry on £300 a year?'

'Why, my dear Mrs Onslow, I think the answer to that is simple. If a young man's betrothed is content to do without the elegancies of life, he is justified in marrying on so small an income, and if not, not. As for steadying a young man's character – it may have that effect if he is of good character already, but I am afraid I doubt whether it will otherwise.'

'But then,' said Louisa, 'to return to your first point, it is not only the elegancies of life. There are unavoidable expenses in marriage – suppose either husband or wife were to fall ill, and require sea air, not to mention a physician's attendance?' She did not like to mention the expense of children, because it was less than two years since, in the space of a week, the Taits had lost all five of their little daughters to scarlet fever.

'Very true,' said the Bishop, who looked to Louisa's eyes as though he were thinking of children. 'What do you for your part consider an adequate income for a young couple, ma'am?'

'I fear I cannot make up my mind, my lord.'

He remarked:

'Sea air can certainly be very expensive – one would never guess it was provided by the Almighty. Are you fond of the seaside, Mrs Onslow?'

'Extremely! Bathing is my delight. But the difficulty of securing a comfortable lodging becomes worse and worse each year. I would not dream of sullying your dinner-table with a description of what Dr Onslow and I had to endure when we were at Ramsgate last summer.'

As Dr Tait guessed, Louisa was referring to bedbugs: he smiled, giving Louisa some idea that while he thought her charming, he did not think her dignified.

Two places along from Louisa, Primrose had turned away from a young lady now being entertained by Mr Newsome, and was talking to the spinster whom Onslow thought looked sensible, but who was in fact given to making disconnected and eccentric remarks. The young lady had been too shy to make good conversation, and caught between two such women, Primrose wished he were in Onslow's place between Mrs Tait and Mrs Reynolds. He always found it easier to talk to married women: spinsters made him wish, a little guiltily, that he desired to be married.

Both Onslow and Primrose were pleased when at length, after dessert, the ladies left the dining room. They stood up with alacrity when Mrs Tait did so, and indulgently watched Louisa smile as the gauze scarf she had dropped was handed to her by Mr Newsome, who appeared to think it as frail as a spider's web. When the last crinoline had been manoeuvred through the dining room door, they sat down again, and waited for the interesting part of the evening to begin.

7

Port was laid on the table, the servants withdrew, and the men moved closer to their host. They talked briefly about the coming abolition of the East India Company, and the French Emperor's ludicrous fear of English assassins, but it was not long before they moved on to discuss a subject which was of far more concern to the four clergymen present. Even the very junior cleric whom Dr Tait had invited to make up the numbers at the last minute was more interested in the new ministry's likely views on high ecclesiastical preferments, and who should fill them, than in French and Indian affairs. The laymen were not so fascinated.

'How good to think that for a while at least we will no longer have Lord Shaftesbury packing the bench with bad scholars and narrow Evangelicals,' said Primrose, finishing his first glass of port. 'It always astonished me that Lord Palmerston listened to him; I suppose it was sheer lack of interest combined with affection made him give Lord Shaftesbury his head.'

'So long as he chose men not likely to vote against the Government in the House of Lords,' said Onslow.

'I think, my dear Primrose,' said Dr Tait, smiling, 'that you are forgetting *I* was one of Lord Palmerston's and Lord Shaftesbury's choices.'

'Tait! My dear fellow, you know perfectly well that I did not mean you. Yours was his one truly admirable appointment – no one in his senses would call you a narrow Evangelical.'

'But I am not so good a scholar as I ought to be.'

Looking at Dr Tait now, Onslow remembered how sixteen years ago, immediately after Dr Arnold's death, they had been rivals competing for the Headmastership of Rugby. He remembered how Tait had been chosen by the trustees even though he was the inferior scholar: Onslow, the Cambridge Senior Classic, had been rejected as too young at twenty-six.

'I only wish I were such a scholar as your lordship,' said the junior cleric.

'Of one thing I'm very sure. Soapy Sam has been hankering after a more important bishopric for I don't know how many years, but there was not a scrap of hope for him while Lord Palmerston remained in office. Oh, I do hope we shall not see him translated to Winchester or Durham, he is intolerable enough as it is, with his mixture of pugnacity and toadying,' said Primrose. Soapy Sam was Samuel Wilberforce, Bishop of Oxford.

'Mr Gladstone wanted to send him to York, Martin, and I am sure was very nearly successful,' Onslow teased. 'Perhaps he will be so when he is back in office, if the Archbishop obliges him by dying in the meantime.'

Primrose went on regardless. 'I detest men with ingratiating manners, and no one has ever been able to discover whether he has any consistent views. I am surprised he did not turn himself almost into a follower of Mr Spurgeon to please Lord Shaftesbury, instead of making a fool of himself with that attempt of his to make adultery a criminal offence. But I suppose I must do him justice: in some respects he has been growing steadily Higher, even though it is contrary to his temporal interests.'

'Very true, alas,' said Dr Tait. He added: 'I must point out, Primrose, that in attacking Lord Palmerston's appointments you find yourself in perfect agreement with the man you so dislike. Does not that appal you?'

'So I do! you are quite right – I must retract my abuse at once. After all,' he said, suddenly grave again, 'it is more important for a bishop to be a good pastor than anything else.'

Dr Tait, as a good host, thought of trying to bring the

46

laymen into this discussion, but he saw they were absorbed in a three-cornered conversation of their own.

'Dr Onslow, what do you think the new ministry is likely to do?' he said.

Onslow gently swung the port in his glass and said:

'It is a pity the Bishops of Oxford and Exeter between them have given both the public and any prospective government a distaste for the mere idea of bishops with High Church sympathies, however vague. I doubt Lord Derby will seek to correct the real imbalance of parties on the bench of bishops – though I daresay he will not prefer even more Evangelicals, Lord Palmerston's policy has been too unpopular.'

'I think you are right in thinking that all parties ought to be represented on the bench,' said Dr Tait, 'but I cannot think of a High Churchman of note who ought to be preferred. Dr Pusey is out of the question.'

'Quite so, my lord,' said Onslow, without denying his real beliefs – he was nothing like so High Church as Dr Pusey.

'It is time Dr Pusey followed Newman to Rome,' struck in the young clergyman. 'He ought not to remain in the Church of England.'

'You are too harsh, Mr Lincoln,' said Dr Tait, making him blush.

'How would Denison do for a High Church bishop?' said Primrose, looking innocent. Onslow raised his eyebrows.

'My dear Martin, what an excellent idea. Yes, he is exactly what we need – another bishop prepared to spend his time taking those who disagree with his views to law with all possible publicity.'

'You are quite right, he would be a second Philpotts,' said Dr Tait, who appeared to have taken Primrose's suggestion seriously. 'I hope we are spared – but in all honesty I cannot think it likely the question will arise.'

'I suppose now that he has been vindicated by the judicial committee there will be no holding him even in Convocation, one dreads to think what he might do in the House of Lords,' said Primrose.

47

'I heard that his parishioners dragged his carriage home themselves after the decision,' said Onslow. 'Is it true, or a mere rumour?'

'True, I believe,' replied Dr Tait. 'I sincerely wish the prosecution had never been begun – he has been made to look a martyr to Low Church and dissenting bigotry, and nothing could be more unfortunate.'

'No, indeed!' said the young clergyman.

Primrose said happily: 'But I am so glad that in spite of the legal decision in his favour the purely doctrinal question remains effectively undecided. I don't mean that I have the least sympathy with the Archdeacon's view of the sacrament or anything else, but latitude is the glory of the Church of England – exactly the view he was trying to combat, of course.'

Dr Tait saw that Onslow was frowning, and said:

'Do you like matters to be a little more clear-cut, Dr Onslow?'

In general, Onslow did: but he was glad that thanks to the muddled case of Archdeacon Denison, it was now possible to hold that the sacrament could be inwardly received by the wicked as well as the faithful. Though he doubted its Anglican legitimacy, that view was a comfort to him. He told Dr Tait:

'It comes of having been a schoolmaster for fourteen years. Latitude and lessons do not mix well – one learns to demand exactness in all things.'

'Oh come,' said Primrose, 'in Dr Arnold's case latitude and lessons mixed perfectly.'

'Martin,' said Onslow suddenly, 'do you never think that even Dr Arnold had his faults?'

'Faults?' said Primrose.

Since the beginning of Primrose's visit to Charton two weeks before, Onslow had listened to constant praise of Arnold, and had agreed with every word of it.

'Yes,' he said. 'Consider his temper – remember March.'

March was a boy whom Arnold had flogged harshly and unjustly in 1832; a scandal had been made of the case in the newspapers.

48

'But – think how noble was his apology, his public apology to him when he discovered he had not lied and it was all a dreadful mistake! The *Northampton Herald* took up the case out of dislike for his politics – you cannot deny it!' exclaimed Primrose.

Onslow looked at the decanter in front of him.

'No, I don't deny it. But he had no business to lose his temper in such a way. A flogging of eighteen strokes is impermissible in even the worst cases.' Like Arthur's incorrigible idleness, he thought, and flushed. The light in the room was too dim for others to notice his changed complexion.

'I agree with you,' said Dr Tait.

'I am glad of it,' Onslow told him.

'None of us is perfect,' said Primrose unwillingly. 'And a hasty temper is a very natural failing – his nature was passionate, not cold like – ' He stopped: he had been about to say 'like yours'. Onslow guessed it, and his lips twisted in a kind of smile. After a moment's pause, he said, finishing his port:

'You must not think I do not reverence him as I ever did. I have tried not to share his faults, but I do not share his virtues either – and if I could only have the half of them, I would willingly have ten times his faults. Believe me.'

'I believe you,' said Primrose.

One of the laymen, a member of Parliament, said:

'I was a fag at Rugby when you and Dr Onslow were in the Sixth, Mr Primrose. A very grubby urchin! I lived in mortal terror of Dr Arnold – and of you.'

All the clergymen were surprised at his entering into the conversation, but Primrose laughed and said politely:

'Oh, surely not!'

'Yes, indeed.'

'So you are inclined to my view?' said Onslow.

'I suppose I might say so, but I never was properly acquainted with him, for I never reached the Sixth.'

Dr Tait, who had found it necessary to curtail the excessive powers of the Sixth when he succeeded Arnold at

Rugby, agreed that neither he nor his system had been flawless. He did not wish to say so, because he had no desire to unsettle Primrose more than he had been unsettled already; therefore, when the conversation began to peter out, he merely said:

'Shall we join the ladies?'

8

The hot sun, made hotter by glass, lent a golden surface to Arthur Bright's brown curls. He took a step away from the window and the light as Onslow handed him his leaving present: a morocco-bound copy of Catullus's poems with an English inscription on the fly-leaf instead of the usual Latin. Onslow's message read: *To Arthur John Bright, on his leaving Charton School, with all kind wishes from his Headmaster. August 7th, 1858.*

'I remembered that you liked Catullus,' he said.

'Yes, sir. Thank you.'

The simple words were spoken in a way that Onslow thought voluptuous. Like Onslow, Bright had never had much to say.

'Do you know, I could wish you had been a better pupil,' Onslow said now, smiling faintly. 'You have parts, but you never cared to use them to the full. I wish – I wish I had been able to interest you in the works of authors other than Ovid and Catullus. But like me, you prefer the Romans to the Greeks, do you not? In so far as you enjoy the classics at all.'

'Yes, sir.'

'It is a rare thing. I could name five men whose preference is for the Greeks for every one who shares our taste.'

Onslow stretched out a hand in the approximate direction of Bright's head, then quickly let it drop. He wanted to say: 'Did you burn all my letters? Promise me that you did,' but he did not. He had never once mentioned his letters, into which he had poured all the emotion which he was too embarrassed to voice in Bright's presence: once they were written, he thrust them from his mind. Only in his very first note, written last November, the first he had ever written to any boy, had he scribbled 'Pray burn this' at the end – he had trusted Bright to treat the others similarly.

'So you are leaving us,' he said aloud.

Bright met his eyes for the first time since he entered the room, and said: 'Yes', without the 'sir'.

Onslow thought the irises of Bright's eyes looked like two translucent, new-fallen horse-chestnuts. It was an image which had occurred to him before.

'Will you ever visit us, do you think?'

'I doubt it, sir. I – '

'You have not been happy here?'

'Happy enough, sir, um, especially this last year in the Sixth,' said Bright. Very occasionally, he would make some remark which showed he had a regard for Onslow.

'My dear boy,' said Onslow, 'you give me pleasure when you tell me that.'

'I am glad,' said Bright, thinking how much he had enjoyed the idea of having the Headmaster in love with him. Love of the idea had always outweighed the discomfort of the reality.

'I hope you will like Trinity. I liked it very well when I was up, though perhaps not quite so much as I had liked Rugby. Of course it will be much changed in many ways since my day. We had a Rugby Debating Society, there were so many of us up from Rugby – it was very enjoyable.'

'I'm sure I shall like it, sir.'

'There seems to be nothing else to say,' said Onslow, turning away. 'Goodbye, Arthur.'

'Goodbye, sir.' Bright put out a hand, but saw against all his expectation that Onslow was unwilling to take it: suddenly it seemed that the Headmaster was treating him like an unclean thing. 'Goodbye!' he said loudly, and went straight to the door, outside which three other boys were waiting to take their final leave of Onslow.

As the door shut behind him, the Headmaster gripped

the back of the nearest chair, closed his eyes, and waited.

═══

Christian Anstey-Ward had received a copy of Plato's *Repbublic* as his leaving-present from Onslow, and the Headmaster's choosing Plato took much of the pleasure out of quitting Charton for good. Christian had come to think of Plato as his private property, or at least as the shared property of himself and a few other, likeminded men whom he had never met, but whom in optimistic moments he dreamt of meeting at Oxford. The idea that Onslow secretly nursed some corrupt version of 'Hellas' was not only intolerable, but frightening. Onslow belonged to the coal- and money-driven world of Queen Victoria's England, out of which nothing but sordidness could be expected to come, towards which no man of sense could have anything but a wearily cynical attitude.

In the five months since he learned about Onslow's relations with Bright, Christian had come to resemble some of his more sophisticated contemporaries. Like them, he imagined that nothing about the world in which he was forced to live could shock him. He no longer looked always anxious, as though perpetually searching for something, and he felt that hard knocks had made him grow a hard shell inside which 'Hellas' could flourish better than before. Yet he feared that by thinking in this way, he had somehow betrayed 'Hellas'. Onslow had forced him to become so cynical about external reality that one day he would become fit for nothing but that reality: his Grecian vision would die.

The day after his last interview with the Headmaster, Christian caught the train from London down to Salisbury. Once on it, he took Onslow's copy of the *Republic* out of his portmanteau, leafed through it, and read a few pages with concentration: but in the end he left it in the railway-carriage, even though he had no copy of his own and meant to buy one.

═══

'Louisa,' said Onslow, making his wife jump, 'shall you miss this garden very much when we leave here?'

'Goodness, Dr Onslow, how you startled me!' She laid down her trowel, tilted her hat back, and looked at him. Then she got to her feet, and Onslow thought that in her huge round hat and short petticoat she looked like nothing so much as a curious toadstool, with a fragile cap and a thick, frilled stalk. She had spent most of the day entertaining parents with Onslow, but her duties had come to an end early enough to allow her half an hour in the garden before it was time for dinner. After the last parents were gone, Onslow had stayed in his study, but then thoughts of Bright drove him to seek the distraction of talking to his wife. 'Why do you ask me such a question? You are not thinking of leaving soon, are you?'

'Not precisely,' said Onslow, though he was. Bright's departure had made him think of it with such panicking seriousness that he thought it worthwhile to drop hints to his wife.

'Shall I miss the garden – well, yes, I shall, but I shall take those plants which can be moved with me.' Louisa's interest was rather in individual plants than in the effect they made when combined in flowerbeds. She had always been a keen botanist, and it amused Onslow to hear her swap long Latin names with fellow enthusiasts. 'You look fagged to death, Dr Onslow.'

'I am certainly tired.'

'The last day of term is always tiring – so many parents wishing to see you without notice.'

'Yes.'

'And having to be unfailingly polite to them is not always the easiest thing in the world.'

'Exactly so.'

Onslow now wished he had not decided to broach the subject of leaving with Louisa, but he had been feeling very much alone. His wife's company and sympathy had seemed better than none, even though it was impossible for her ever to understand.

'Dr Onslow, why this sudden mention of leaving? Is it only that you are worn out?'

'Yes, only that.' He hesitated: the temptation to speak was still there. 'But after all, you will own that I cannot remain a headmaster all my life.'

'No, of course not. Another five years, perhaps?' said Louisa, delighted that Onslow was consulting her as though she were an adult person. In another five years Onslow would still be under fifty: the perfect age for a new bishop.

'Perhaps. Yet I believe I have already accomplished the work God sent me to do here, as well as I can.'

'Indeed, you have accomplished it very well – better than anyone else could have done, I am sure.'

'No, Louisa, many others would have done far better than I.'

'Stuff!' she said.

'I wish you would not use such unladylike expressions. Do you pick them up from the boys?' As he said this, Onslow drew Louisa's arm through his own, and studied her little hand in its brown leather gardening glove. Then he removed the glove, and caressed the bare hand because it was his legitimate property. He thought of Bright, whom he had tried to give up before the final break yesterday – but it had been as though he were a drunkard asked to abstain while there was a bottle of spirits on the table in front of him.

Louisa watched his exploring hand, and curled her fingers. Onslow thought that if Bright could be compared to a bottle of brandy, Louisa could be compared to one of her own plants – one of the less unusual and more colourful plants. She was Primrose's sister, and she did not repel him. It was not always necessary to think of her as his own little sister by adoption. He liked the fact that she was so small, and rather too slim for a woman. The softness of her body was as pleasant and inessential as a rose.

Onslow's sudden idea of retiring, retreating, escaping from what he loved, began to fade.

'No, I do not think there is any need for me to go just

55

yet,' he said, thinking that now Bright was gone, with Louisa's help, he would resist temptation. He tipped his wife's chin up, pushed off her hat, and dryly kissed her lips.

9

Christian Anstey-Ward had spent his childhood in Weymouth, where his father had a lucrative medical practice, but since 1856 his family had lived at Poplar House, outside Wilton near Salisbury. Dr Anstey-Ward had inherited both the house and a fortune amounting to about £800 a year from an uncle, who had left everything to him on condition that he add the name of Ward to his own. This had been a wholly unexpected piece of good fortune, for Dr Anstey had only once met his reclusive uncle and never imagined he would inherit anything.

Dr Anstey had saved a considerable sum during his working life and had invested it cautiously in the three-percent Consols. His total income after he inherited old Mr Ward's estate was therefore enough to enable him to retire in comfort to Poplar House, and devote all his time to his hobbies of geology, palaeontology and natural history. His unmarried sister, Christian's Aunt Chatty, had hoped that they would make a social move as well as a geographical one, into county society, but this had not happened. Dr Anstey-Ward was the son of a coal-merchant, and though he enjoyed having the leisure of a country gentleman, he disliked society nearly as much as his uncle had, and was therefore not much interested in social advancement for himself. But he had a certain wish to see his son enter the upper class, largely because Christian, he thought, was not well suited to any business or profession except perhaps that of an Oxford don.

'Well, my son, it's good to have you back,' Dr Anstey-Ward said when Christian arrived home, early in the evening of the day he left Charton. 'And what do you mean to do with yourself till October?'

'To read, mostly, Father – in preparation for Oxford.'

'None of your friends has asked you to stop with him for a while, or perhaps go on a walking tour, or anything of that nature, eh?' said Dr Anstey-Ward, who knew that Christian had very few friends. 'I should have supposed you'd done enough reading at Charton.'

'No, sir.'

'Well, so long as you are content, Christian. Now, where can your aunt be, and Rose?' he said, turning away.

At that moment, Christian's aunt opened the drawing-room door, and briskly walked over to embrace him. She was tall and stout, like her brother and her niece. Christian, who took after his dead mother, was the only delicate-looking member of the family, just as he was the only one at all interested in the beauty of his surroundings, or the lack of it – the mixture of conventional modern taste and drab utilitarian objects which he saw in his father's house was a source of pain to him.

'Christian!' said Chatty. 'You are not looking as well as you ought. Charton is supposed to be so healthily situated.'

'It is only the effects of travelling, Aunt Chatty. How are you?'

'Very well indeed. As soon as I heard you arrive I went to fetch Rose out of that dark-room of hers, but she insists she cannot leave it even for you – those nasty wet plates or whatever they may be are in a critical condition, so she says.' Rose was Christian's only surviving, elder sister. He had no brothers. 'Your father continues to encourage her – he gave her a new camera for her birthday, and I'm told it uses quick exposure, but all I can say is that quick or not, it doesn't make Rose waste less time in the dark-room.'

'Now, my dear Chatty, it's no more a waste of time than other young ladies' hobbies, dried flowers and the like,' said Dr Anstey-Ward.

'Other young ladies do not enter the presence of gentlemen smelling of chemicals.'

'We can't be squabbling about Rose when Christian has

58

but just come back. How did you leave Dr Onslow, my boy?'

Christian flushed. 'In excellent health, sir.'

'Good. Good.'

Christian knew that in spite of his having just returned home, in spite of the welcome he had received, his father and aunt were more interested in his sister than in him. He prepared to listen to further discussion of her habits, especially her photography.

Rose's photography was a source of dissension between Dr Anstey-Ward and his sister because both were agreed that such a messy and mildly eccentric hobby would be a bar to her marriage. Her father had no wish for Rose to marry, because he did not want to be left alone with Chatty, with whom he had not much in common. For this reason, he bound his daughter to him with expensive gifts of photographic equipment, always implying when he made them that no husband would indulge her similarly. Chatty, on the other hand, did wish Rose to be married, because long ago, she had wanted to marry herself.

Christian did not perceive that his sister's position was a difficult one; he only saw that she was the favourite.

'What have you been doing, Aunt Chatty?' he said, as Dr Anstey-Ward left the room. It seemed he was not to listen to a long talk about Rose after all.

'For the most part, trying my best to reduce the scandal caused by your father's never going to church,' she told him.

'But you and Rose go to church every Sunday,' said Christian, surprised.

'Rose attends only morning service now. And despite all my training she has no reverence whatever for the Sabbath – sees no harm in messing with her camera or reading a novel after church, and of course your father never interferes. I believe he would like her to be a professed infidel.'

'Perhaps he would,' said Christian, hoping that his aunt would not be able to make him go to church twice on Sundays, now that he was no longer a schoolboy. It occurred to him that he could please his father by saying

59

that he had lost his faith, though he had not so much lost it as had a large part of it rubbed out by Onslow, and he did not want to talk about that.

'But so far as our neighbours are concerned, Rose's behaviour scarcely signifies: it is the religious opinions of a household's head that are of real importance. I can subscribe to foreign missions, and help circulate tracts, but still Mr Eames will look at me askance.' Mr Eames was the vicar. 'Though to be sure he is always very civil.'

Listening to Chatty, Christian felt his spirits rise a little. It seemed that though he was not the chief object of affection or even of temporary interest, he had at least become accepted as an adult – someone to whom his aunt would criticise his father, and his father criticise his aunt. He wondered whether Rose, who was four years his senior, would also stop treating him as a boy. Somehow, he found it difficult to harbour a true Greek contempt for women when women did not look up to him as a man. He was very sure that the women of 'Hellas' bowed down before the wisdom even of boys, and he never could quite accustom himself to the fact that in the *Symposium*, the all-wise tutor of Socrates was Diotima, an undoubted female.

——

One day in mid August, when Dr Anstey-Ward was up in London showing an unusual fossil to the curator of the Natural History section of the British Museum, Christian drove into Salisbury with his aunt and sister. The two women were to call on the wife of one of the prebendaries, but Christian excused himself, and instead wandered alone down a dark little street not far from the cathedral close. There he found a bookseller's shop which he had not noticed before, and he went in and glanced idly round the dim interior.

His eyes were caught not by a book, but by a young boy's short veil of falling hair, framed by a shaft of light. The boy was kneeling on the floor, unpacking a crate full of second-hand volumes, and his head was bent over the pages of one of them. His finger was tracing the words, and the trembling of his lower lip, faint as that of a leaf on a windless day, showed like his pointing finger that he was unused to reading. Yet Christian saw that he was drinking in the words with eager if puzzled concentration, scanning them with a haste which showed his fear that his employer might surprise him. He had not noticed Christian's entrance.

The boy's white-golden hair concealed his eyes, but his short, bare upper lip, his square yet delicate cleft chin, and his straight nose could all be seen. There was something about the curve of his lips, combined with his interest in the book, which made Christian think: this must be he. He wanted the boy to lift his head and show his eyes more than he wanted anything else in the world, but he dared say nothing to disturb him.

Instead, without distaste, he noticed the boy's ill-fitting, dark clerk's clothes, and the roughness and redness of his small but strongly-shaped hands, which seemed only to heighten by contrast the perfection of his appearance as a whole. He was slim and graceful, with beautifully proportioned shoulders and waist. He was too pale and cool to look like a mere cherub, in spite of his yellow hair.

At last Christian said: 'What is it you are reading?' in a voice which was little more than a whisper, but which seemed to him to make an immense ripple in the still air of the shop. The boy started, and scrambled to his feet, snapping the book shut with one hand and pushing the hair off his white forehead with the other. He looked Christian full in the face, seemed to swallow once or twice, and then said:

'It's poetry, sir.'

Christian saw that his eyes were neither blue nor grey, but of a rich hazel, long and large, set under blond brows as clear and firm as the mouldings on a coin. They were as fine as, finer than, he had dared to hope, and the boy's slow Dorset accent was something far removed from the vulgarly whining chirrup he had dreaded might come from between those lips.

61

Without saying anything, Christian put out his hand for the book, which the other gave him willingly. Their fingertips met. He saw that it was a scarcely-worn copy of Mrs Browning's *Aurora Leigh*. His thoughts were not on the poem, though he had been meaning to read it himself, but on the fact that a boy whose appearance might have been designed with him in mind, who made the grey-eyed Greek beloved of his dreams look insipid, was flesh. His hands began to sweat with nervousness as he held the open book: then an idea came to him. He opened his mouth, about to say: 'I'll buy this for you, if you would like it,' but at that moment the door was opened by a woman.

Suddenly he realised that to say such a thing would be crazy, almost wicked. He put the book quickly down on a table and dodged round the woman's crinoline, out into the street.

It was some days before he dared go back. He lay awake at night wondering in hope and fear what the angel in the shop had thought of his behaviour and his looks, imagining he could never bring himself to try again. But the acquaintance was made in time, and on his very next visit he found out that the boy's name was Jemmy Baker, that he was just sixteen, that he lived with his widowed mother, and that he loved poetry for its musical sounds.

10

It was a Sunday morning towards the end of September, and the Anstey-Wards were gathered round the breakfast-table in front of a french window, which stood wide open although the day was a little chilly. Rose, Christian and Chatty were dressed for church, but Dr Anstey-Ward, never having gone since he abandoned his practice in Weymouth, was not. His sister thought that whatever his beliefs, he ought not to flaunt them by dressing in weekday clothes on the Sabbath.

'I shall not be here for dinner,' Christian said, helping himself to tea. 'If no one else is planning to use it, I would be glad to have the dog-cart.'

'You don't mean to say you're going to spend the whole of Sunday with that little shop-walker in Salisbury again?' said his aunt. 'And miss afternoon service, I don't doubt?'

'Yes, I can see him for any length of time only on Sundays, you know, because his hours are very long,' Christian replied. His tone was tranquil, soft even, because he was talking about Jemmy. He had not concealed his interest in Jemmy after his family began to ask questions about his frequent trips to Salisbury, because his interest in him was entirely chaste.

Dr Anstey-Ward's heavy eyebrows drew together.

'This is the fourth Sunday you have missed dining with us, Christian. I don't like it. A piece of cold pie as a luncheon and a bite of supper are not sustaining enough for a boy of your age – and you don't eat enough, even when you are here. It puzzles me that the tonic I prescribed has not done you more good – too much quinine perhaps.'

Christian had lost his appetite, which had never been good, since the excitement of meeting Jemmy. He said:

'Perhaps we could dine rather later than usual? Then perhaps I could be here.'

'I've no wish to keep London hours,' said his father, a little peevishly. 'Five o'clock is the time for a heavy meal: a later hour hinders good digestion.'

'It is very old-fashioned, Father,' said Rose. 'I've heard that even in some of the colleges at Cambridge dinner in hall is now at six.'

'Oh? And how do you come to know so much about Cambridge, miss?'

'Mr Charlie Ibbotson happened to mention it.'

'Well Christian,' said Anstey-Ward, taking no notice of his daughter's reply, 'if we dine at six today – providing that your aunt finds it perfectly convenient – can you be with us?'

Very unwillingly, because he had been sure that dinner would not be postponed on his account, Christian said yes. 'And may I take the dog-cart into Salisbury?' The dog-cart was the Anstey-Wards' only carriage.

'You took it last Sunday,' said his sister. 'Aunt Chatty and I want it today.'

'Very well,' said Christian, setting down his cup. 'Then if I'm to be in time for the cathedral service I must go now.'

The thought that Jemmy would be waiting faithfully for him in the cathedral's limpid gloom, ready to share his hymn-book, scarcely compensated him for this disappointment. He had looked forward for days to driving Jemmy out to where they could walk along the banks of the Avon or the Bourne, as they had done only once before. It was so much easier to clasp Jemmy's hand and tell him that he loved him out in the wild than in the cathedral close, where all he could do, somehow, was earnestly describe Plato and 'Hellas' and the true theory of love as they walked round and round. Jemmy had been more at ease in the country. So often he looked rather bewildered: though always pleased and flattered by the attentions of so clever and kind

64

a young man, whom he said, when pressed, he liked very much.

Just as Christian pushed his chair back, his father did the same.

'That boy is not a suitable friend for you, Christian,' Anstey-Ward said.

'So I have been saying this age past!' said Chatty. 'A boy who is not even a clerk, merely a shop-walker – it's the most eccentric, provoking thing I ever heard of. When I think of the money it cost to send you to Charton – '

'Is that what you mean, sir?' said Christian, looking from his aunt's ruddy face to his father's. 'That Jemmy and I belong to different classes of society?'

Anstey-Ward looked steadily at him.

'I fancy a close friendship with a boy so far beneath you socially can one way and another do you little good, though I don't deny he seems an amiable lad. Your aunt is right, Christian, it is very eccentric.' He added: 'That doesn't, to be sure, make it wrong, but surely there are equally likeable young men of your own age and rank to be found.'

'Jemmy Baker has a – purity of mind which it seems to me it is impossible to find among the upper classes, certainly if most Charton boys are representative – and their masters too,' said Christian, looking out of the window. 'I am glad you acknowledge that there can be no real harm in my being friends with Jemmy.'

'That is not precisely what I said, my boy,' said Anstey-Ward. 'But I do acknowledge that I had rather you had a taste for low company, so long as it were not morally low, than were a mere tuft-hunter.'

'Thank you, Father,' said Christian. He excused himself to his aunt and sister, and then left the room.

━━━

After breakfast, in his library, Anstey-Ward took a large bag of fossils from his last collecting trip out of the cupboard, and began to label and catalogue them. He already possessed a vast collection, which he housed in specially made drawers, and sometimes he thought he ought to refrain from adding further specimens unless they were truly exceptional – but the idea was not attractive. Gathering and ordering fossils was a great pleasure to him, a pleasure that not even Rose could understand. There was also the consideration that his days were rather empty, and must be filled with constructive activity.

Though he had a rigid schedule to which he kept conscientiously, Anstey-Ward was not an effective worker. With his grizzled hair, shrewd eyes and portly figure, he looked to be extremely solid, but his was in fact a grasshopper mind. He had achieved little by his scientific researches because, like his son, he found it difficult to concentrate for a long time on any one thing, and would constantly skip from one area of research to another, usually giving his attention directly to the large question rather than adding his mite to the small factual details which ran down and accumulated in the hour-glass of theory – or failed to do so. He did not even confine himself to the wide fields of palaeontology and geology, but had at various times been chiefly interested in mesmerism, in phrenology, and in the attempt to produce primitive forms of life out of inorganic matter by the use of electricity.

Just at present, Anstey-Ward was attempting to concentrate on something small and specialised. He was interested in theories of the transmutation of species, and it was his aim to discover a fossil which would be hard evidence in favour of an idea which he had found deeply intriguing, but only a shade less unlikely than that of a multitude of separate creations in each succeeding geological period. But so far, he had searched in vain for an obviously transitional form of life, and he was beginning to consider making a study of the mating habits of snails.

As he worked at his labelling, Anstey-Ward found himself thinking about Christian, of whom he considered himself to be very fond, yet with whom he could never have a thoroughly comfortable conversation. In his mind there was a picture of the boy he hoped to see in a year's time, after Oxford had begun to do its work: a boy cured of shyness, of weak lungs, of eccentricity, and of vagueness about his future. He did not doubt that Christian would be happier at Oxford than he had been at Charton, and he believed that happiness could work wonders. The boy might even develop an interest in science, and be able to argue with his father in a friendly way – Anstey-Ward, though moderately reclusive, loved to argue with both friends and enemies, and he rarely had the chance to do either.

And, thought Anstey-Ward, fingering an ammonite, Christian's odd friendship with the little bookseller's assistant would certainly come to an end.

11

In the summer of 1859, Christian sat with Jemmy Baker under a willow-tree, sheltered from the sun's glare by the layered curtain of its leaves. The river Avon flowed by like moving glass, and all else around them was still in the heat-haze – only a few crickets cheeped in the grass. The two young men sprawled with their coats off, their collars loosened, and their boots discarded, but they were still distressingly hot.

A year at Oxford had strengthened Christian, and given him both new friends and intellectual food, but it had not altered his feelings for Jemmy as his father hoped. Jemmy's beauty, like Charton's moral and physical squalor, remained constantly in his mind – as much at Oxford as in the vacations, when he had little to do. He wanted never to forget Jemmy, but he wished he could rid himself of all memories of Charton. It amazed him that in what ought to have been his present contentment, he could not stop thinking about the corruption he had seen there, and wondering precisely what it was Onslow and Bright had done together. Sometimes it crossed his mind that perhaps there had been nothing but a few kisses between them, but the words of Onslow's note, hot as the day, seemed to make that unlikely. Christian still kept the three pieces of paper he had received nearly eighteen months ago: Bright's note in chapel, Bright's letter, Onslow's extract.

Jemmy was, in his own fashion, as disturbing as memories of Charton. Even after a year's friendship, he was wholly passive; he initiated nothing. He wrote short letters to Christian at Oxford only when Christian begged him, and never seemed really to understand the nature of the love which Christian explained. But he said that he liked to receive Christian's letters, and he was still prepared to give up the greater part of his Sundays to him during the vacations. He admired Christian greatly, and was anxious to get on in the world: to this end Christian was teaching him a little Latin, at his own request.

This was the first Sunday of the Long Vacation, and Christian had not seen Jemmy for over two months.

'I am so glad to have been able to see you before I leave for Switzerland,' he said.

'Oh, yes. You'll be away a long time, shan't you?' said Jemmy.

'A month. Yes, quite a long time – I wish you might come too.' Christian was to join a combined walking and reading party in the Swiss Alps, headed by two Fellows of his college, one of whom was a founder member of the Alpine Club, while the other looked forward to reading Romantic poems aloud in suitable natural surroundings as much as to exploring Greek texts. 'If it had not been for seeing you, I would have remained in London till our party leaves,' continued Christian.

'Would you, sir?' In general, Jemmy called Christian nothing, but occasionally a 'sir' slipped out.

'Don't call me sir, Jemmy. I wonder why you find it so hard to say Christian.'

'I don't know. It doesn't feel like the right thing, precisely. I don't know why.'

'What a foolish boy you are.'

Christian rolled over on his stomach, and smelt the hay-like grass. Then he raised his head.

'Why don't we bathe?'

'Bathe?' said Jemmy stupidly. 'But you can only bathe in the sea.'

'Wherever did you get such a notion? At Oxford everyone bathes in the river – surely you have done so before?'

'I can't swim.'

'That's of no importance, the water's not deep. Don't you wish to?'

Jemmy said:

'Maybe, but someone might see us.'

'Oh, that's hardly likely, this is a very secluded place. Come.' Christian got up, and took off his waistcoat and necktie.

'They'd think it wrong, if they did see.'

'Jemmy, there is nothing wrong, immoral, about nakedness. All the athletes were naked in Greece.' Christian's heart beat fast as he said this.

'We're not living in Greece,' said Jemmy. He added: 'And I was not thinking of being naked, I was thinking of the fish. They'd say we were disturbing the fish.'

Christian, surprised by this, merely said:

'No one will see, I'm sure of it.' He wanted to say something to the effect that despite mere appearances, they were living in Greece, but somehow found it difficult, as he never had before.

'I don't know,' Jemmy told him.

'Surely you know that not a soul has come near us since we got here,' said Christian, a little impatiently. 'Well, even if you won't bathe, I shall.' He unbuttoned his trousers, and stood before Jemmy in his shirt-tails. His ruffled, flyaway hair made a shaggy halo round his head. Then he removed his shirt and undershirt and stood naked. His figure was not beautiful, but it was better than his face: its only real fault was that it was too thin.

'Come Jemmy,' he said.

'Very well, if you want,' said the other; and slowly, with lowered eyes, he began to undress.

Christian did not watch this process, because he sensed that Jemmy did not want him to. Instead, he made his way down the short bank and through the fringe of riverside plants, into the cool of the water. Sharply sucking in his breath, he flopped down into it, and performed a few breast-strokes. A mental picture of white nude Jemmy was constantly before his eyes as he waited for the reality to appear. Suddenly he thought: I'll teach him to swim. Now Christian saw himself holding Jemmy up in the water.

'Is it very cold?'

Christian turned quickly, and then saw that Jemmy still had his shirt on.

'It's delightful. Take your shirt off!'

Rather roughly, Jemmy obeyed him, and cast the shirt away. He stood there with his arms dangling uncomfortably, and a faint breeze lifting his hair. Then at last Christian saw that his figure was just as he had imagined: there before him were the square shoulders, the slim hips and the little bottom all as white as a white-fleshed peach. Jemmy's penis was not large, but was well-shaped and well-coloured, surrounded by light brown hair. Christian glanced at it, then raised his eyes quickly to the boy's face, though an image of it remained in his mind.

'Let me teach you to swim,' he said, wading forward, showing his own ruddy penis above the water-line. The river was less than four feet deep even in the middle, and Christian knew it was not the best place for learning to swim. But it would do.

'If you like.' Jemmy trod uncertainly towards the river, disliking the feel of plants under his bare feet.

'Plunge in,' said Christian, wanting to pull him into the water.

'Ooh! It's cold.'

Jemmy did not plunge in, but climbed doggedly down. Having agreed to bathe, he thought it would be cowardly to withdraw only because the water was colder than he had expected, but he wished he had never said yes.

'Shall I teach you how to swim?' said Christian again. 'I'll have to hold you up in the water.'

Jemmy, who had just forced himself to dip his head in, gazed at him out of eyes covered with fronds of hair-like pale seaweed.

'Will you?' he said, pushing his hair back.

'You look like a male Nereid. Yes, I shall have to hold you, just at first.' Christian gripped the slimy pebbles of the riverbed with his toes, put a hand on either side of Jemmy's taut waist, and clasped it. 'Now lie flat on your stomach,' he said. 'Imagine you are in bed. There. Let your legs rise up, the water will hold them.'

71

Jemmy managed to do as he was told, but had trouble keeping his face out of the water. 'Paddle the water with your hands, and kick your legs,' said Christian, still holding on tightly to Jemmy's waist. 'You're swimming! I'm going to release my grip, very slowly . . .' As soon as he did so, Jemmy gave way to temptation, and planted his feet back on the riverbed. Then he slipped, and went right under, and came up spluttering.

Christian laughed; not in mockery, even kind mockery, but out of happiness. After a second or two, Jemmy copied him. 'I don't think I'm just cut out for swimming,' he said.

'Nonsense! We could try again.'

'No, thank'ee.'

'Very well,' said Christian. 'But are you not enjoying the water?'

'It's passable, after being so hot.'

They spent some ten minutes in the river, dipping and paddling, and shyly flicking water at each other, laughing as they did so. Then Jemmy decided he was growing cold, and Christian followed him out.

'We must allow the sun to dry us before we put on our clothes,' he said. To be naked with Jemmy on the grass, he thought, would be better even than being naked with him in the river. He planned to weave a wreath of flowers, and place it on Jemmy's head, and call him a shepherd of Arcadia.

'Pity we didn't think to bring towels.'

'Yes,' said Christian, speaking uncertainly.

Jemmy seemed to have lost all self-consciousness about being naked. He stood stretching upwards, yawning, his flanks adorned with drops of water; and Christian stared at him. New feelings were roused in him, but old words came to his lips.

'Do you know how very beautiful you are?' As he said this, Christian stepped forward, and laid a finger, then a hand, on the small of Jemmy's back. 'You have come straight to me from out of ancient Hellas.'

Christian's penis, soft and gentle throughout their time in the river, was now quite suddenly raised and huge.

'Let me kiss you.'

Jemmy felt the active penis brush against him. He had never rejected the light kisses Christian planted on his forehead, never objected to praise of his beauty, and Christian now waited, breathing stertorously, with his eyes narrowed and his face flushed.

'If you want to kiss someone, you ought to kiss a girl.' Jemmy moved away from Christian's hand, which had descended from his back to the upper slope of his right buttock.

'Jemmy!' Gasping, Christian saw that the boy's own penis was erect, almost fully erect as he struggled into his drawers. 'Jemmy.'

'I don't want to kiss you, that's all.'

'But I can tell you do!'

'I don't!' Jemmy pulled on his trousers and buttoned them, and after a moment, Christian realised that he too must put on his clothes, wet and shaking though he was.

When they were both dressed, he said to Jemmy:

'If I have offended you, will you forgive me?'

'Yes,' said Jemmy, not looking at him.

'You will still be my friend?'

'Yes, but I'd like to go home now.'

Christian did not believe that he was forgiven. He was sure that Jemmy would seek to avoid him now, sure that he had ruined everything by one sudden piece of Charton-like behaviour. The drive back to Salisbury was silent, and when they reached Jemmy's mother's lodgings, Jemmy confirmed Christian's suspicions by jumping out of the dog-cart without offering his hand for a squeeze or his forehead for a peck. It was the end, thought Christian.

12

To Christian, the thought that he had behaved like Onslow was almost worse than the thought that Jemmy would no longer wish to see him. He had believed that he was incapable of feeling simple lust, that his need to worship a beautiful boy had everything to do with the Ideal and nothing to do with the penis. It was true that in 'Hellas' there was physical love, but Christian believed that it was somehow quite a different thing from the sexual indulgences of Charton boys, especially the indulgences of Onslow and Bright. It was a more passionate version of the keen chaste love he had felt for Jemmy till that blazing day, a holy celebration of nudity such as he had tried and failed to make.

In the few days before he left for Switzerland, Christian tried to persuade himself that the desires he felt beside the Avon had also been a glorious and noble thing, but accustomed though he was to self-deceit, he was unable to do so. It was all too recent, he could remember it too clearly, he knew too well it was not love of the heavenly Ideal he felt, not when Jemmy's penis had been erect too. And yet Jemmy had rightly, despite his own involuntary excitement, rejected him for betraying 'Hellas'.

The dark Onslow-self inside him must be rooted out and crushed — like Onslow, who must be responsible for its growing inside him.

Although when he went abroad Christian had no conscious plan of what to do with it, he took the evidence against his

74

old headmaster with him to Switzerland. For several days he took it out whenever he was alone, and contemplated it – it seemed to him that if he were not careful, he would one day express himself in similar terms, and talk of sofas rather than of Plato. He thought of how he had treasured these pieces of paper, and yet till now had never thought of taking any action – he had been able to ignore the sordidness of others' lives. When Bright first made his revelation, it had not once occurred to him to send the incriminating pieces of paper to Charton's trustees, or anything of that kind. He had accepted Bright's demand that he keep silence, and had merely become a cynic.

Even now, Christian wondered whether he were capable of taking any kind of action. Mixed with his increased hatred of Onslow's memory there was a new, distinct sympathy for him, the sympathy of one who could understand the power of unwanted impulses: but when he thought of giving way to this sympathy, and maintaining silence, Christian felt panic. To continue helping conceal the evil, as Bright had made him swear he would, would be to send himself down the criminal path at the end of which 'Hellas' was a brothel. He needed to teach himself what happened to men who corrupted the sweetest of dreams, yet after many days and nights of worrying, he could not decide whether he had a real right to act.

In the end, after he had been abroad for a week, Christian decided that he would explain a part of the situation and seek advice. He reviewed his acquaintance with considerable care, and the man he at length chose to confide in was Mr Fergus Mildmay, one of the Fellows of Magdalen who had organised the trip to Switzerland.

Mr Mildmay was a don who seemed to regard undergraduates not as the drawback to an academic life, but as one of its chief pleasures. He and Christian had had several discussions about Greek art and philosophy, the *Phaedrus* and the *Symposium*, and understood each other very well. No mentor could have been more different from Onslow than Mr Mildmay, thought Christian – and yet, Mildmay was also a clergyman, and interested in young men. He was tall and ugly, with a gentle tongue and a kind heart, but rigid principles.

One morning when all other members of their party were out on the mountain, Christian told Mildmay that he was in sore need of advice, and then haltingly explained his dilemma: Bright had sworn him to secrecy, yet he could not be sure that in such a case as this, it was right to keep his word. He then described the case as delicately as he could, without looking Mildmay in the eye. Mildmay listened to him in astonished silence, asking only whether or not he had proof, and then, forgetting the sprained ankle which had recently confined him to the house, he jumped up. At last he said, staring across at the mountains and nursing his foot:

'My dear Anstey-Ward, I cannot tell you, cannot tell you, how sorry I am. God bless my soul! That you should have discovered your own headmaster, a doctor of divinity, in such a – a – I cannot find words to express it. No, indeed!' 'God bless my soul' was the strongest expression Mildmay ever used.

'But what am I to do, sir?' said Christian. 'It has been preying on my conscience for so long. I suppose I ought not to have consulted you, because of course to do so I had to break Bright's trust in me, but I know that if you think I ought to keep his trust from now on you won't say a word more about it.'

'No, no! It is your positive duty to break the poor boy's trust, Anstey-Ward, in such a case as this.'

There was a long pause. Christian felt oddly cold and flat now that he had confessed Onslow's sin instead of his own – he thought of Jemmy, whom he had of course not mentioned, and wondered what would happen. He had suspected that Mildmay would not say he must keep his word to Bright, but the consideration that Bright had spoken in confidence had nonetheless weighed quite heavily with him: for eighteen months he had accepted the school-boy code of honour with regard to not telling tales, and it had been hard to release himself from it, even under the pressure of his own needs.

'When you say it is my duty to break his trust,' he said slowly at last, as Mr Mildmay continued to shake his head to himself in private distress, 'do you mean for the sake of the boys at Charton – the very bad effect Dr Onslow has had on them?' He continued quickly: 'I saw things which I don't like to describe to you – the endemic moral corruption – it was everywhere.' He wanted to talk about this very much, quite as much as about Onslow.

Mildmay stared at him. 'Dr Onslow's personal failings are inexcusable, but yet that does not mean he has not been an admirable schoolmaster. He is celebrated, justly so, for the moral reformation which he has wrought at Charton!'

Christian was astonished by Mildmay's seeming unwillingness to believe in the appalling state of Charton, in view of the way in which he had quickly been persuaded that Onslow himself had enjoyed a love-affair with a pupil. The mere mention of written proof had been enough. Then he remembered that Mildmay had been educated by tutors, not at a public school, till he went up to Oxford.

'As far as this is concerned,' he said, 'there has been no reformation, I promise you.'

Mildmay licked his lips, unable to tolerate the pictures of dormitory orgies that sprang into his mind. 'I cannot – cannot believe – I think the question is rather that a clergyman of the Church of England has shown himself in the most shocking way to be unfit to hold his office. Anstey-Ward, no consideration of – of what I might call merely worldly standards of honour, of confidence and so forth, ought to hold you back from exposing him. I am very, very sorry for it, but indeed it is your duty now to act against him!'

'Exposing him? Publicly?' cried Christian, suddenly appalled. 'But I can't, sir – I can't! I could not take any action – what action? writing to *The Times* – to the trustees, the Prime Minister? You must see it's impossible!' He could not bear the suggestion that he might bring Onslow down personally, and in the most brutal possible way. Even though he had briefly considered doing it, he knew now it would have to be someone else, someone who had never

77

been his pupil and did not share his passion, preferably Mildmay.

Mildmay said sternly: 'Will you not even demand privately that he resign? He cannot be allowed to remain in an honourable position and one moreover where he is exposed to temptation. Even though he has done much good – '

'He has done no good!'

'If that were true it would be all the more reason to oblige him to retire.'

Breathing quickly, they watched each other.

'Oh, my dear Anstey-Ward,' said the other, suddenly relaxing and placing a hand on his knee. 'Forgive me. I think I understand. You have hesitated for so long and are now so reluctant very largely because you held Dr Onslow in peculiar reverence and affection, did you not? You felt for him that love of a pupil for a wise master, and the discovery that he had feet of clay, I might almost say of, er, *effluent* – ' he laughed nervously, tapping Christian's knee with his fingernail – 'was indescribably painful to you? No wonder the thought of doing as I suggested is abhorrent to you. It does credit to your heart, whatever else.'

Christian looked at him dumbly as this misunderstanding grew to gigantic proportions in Mildmay's mind.

'But you see,' continued Mildmay, 'the fact that you love him does not make it less necessary that he be at least removed – perhaps not publicly exposed and disgraced, no. I was allowing anger to overcome me, when I suggested that.'

'No,' said Christian in a low voice.

'I think that what you should do is simply to inform your father. Dr Anstey-Ward is well able to handle so delicate and painful a situation on your behalf. Bless my soul, yes indeed! You will have discharged your duty in telling him. I cannot think either God or man would require you to involve yourself more closely in something so deeply distressing to you.'

Christian's sense of what was honest was keen enough to force him to say: 'I didn't love Onslow, sir, as master or – or anything else – I almost hate him for what he has done.'

This Mr Mildmay took as proof of such pure love as he would have liked to receive himself from all his students. He sighed, his hand still on Christian's knee and his eyes on the wide water of Lake Brienz.

'Write to your father, Anstey-Ward, and send him the notes you possess. Trust him to do what is right. Do this – please do this.'

Christian said nothing.

'You must. I do assure you that you must.'

'Yes,' said Christian eventually. 'I suppose so.' Though he spoke with such hesitation, he saw that a tolerable solution had been found, thanks to Mildmay's horrible mistake.

'Do you have the letters here?' said Mildmay, leaning forward. 'No, I suppose you cannot have. It will have to wait until we are back in England.'

'Yes, I do have them – they're in my portmanteau, upstairs.'

'Then write from here, enclosing them,' said Mildmay. 'If I can be of any assistance – to you or to your father, pray, pray do not hesitate to ask me.'

'Thank you. I don't doubt you've given me very good advice. I don't know what my father will do, perhaps nothing, but it will be his decision – I shall tell him what you think.'

Christian got up from the bench where they were sitting, and went into the house. Having thrown the pebble to start a moral avalanche, he was walking like a drunken man.

13

My dear Father, wrote Christian in the final draft of his letter to Anstey-Ward, *I hope this letter finds you well, and Rose and Aunty Chatty also. Pray give them my best love.*

For my part, I am enjoying both the scenery and the climate here, and the cough which was troubling me in England appears to have departed, for which I am thankful. I take pleasure also in the company of those who are with me, in particular that of Mr Mildmay, whom you will perhaps remember meeting, and liking, when you visited me at Oxford in April. We have enjoyed many quiet discussions about Plato and Theocritus since we arrived here, neither of us being quite so fond of mountain-walking as our companions – including Mr Dixon, who is one of the Alpine Club's keenest members.

I have, as you will hear, especial cause to be grateful to Mr Mildmay, for he has advised me about a delicate and painful matter, which I must now (on his advice) confide to you. How I wish I might entertain you with a description of the Alps instead! Forgive me, pray, for consulting him first, instead of going directly to you – I think when you have read this letter you will understand why it was less difficult for me to go first to a comparative stranger for advice than to my father.

How difficult it is to know where to begin, when I know that what I have to say will grieve you. For over a year now, this question has been troubling me greatly, for it was impossible to know where my real duty lay. I was sworn to secrecy and I have, of course, several scruples about breaking the promise I gave to him who entrusted me with

80

his confidence. Yet always I have wondered whether in such a case as this it was right to abide by my promise, for the confidence reposed in me by my friend concerns something that may be a crime and is certainly a violation of the moral law, committed by one who ought to be one of its foremost guardians: my old headmaster Dr Onslow.

I have now to tell you plainly, after this preliminary, that Dr Onslow formed a shameful connection with a friend of mine, Arthur Bright, while we were both in the Sixth at Charton − I enclose proof of an assertion which you will no doubt find incredible with this letter. At first, I naturally refused to believe what Bright told me about himself and Dr Onslow, but ever since he showed me these papers (in February of last year) I have found it impossible to be anything but wretched. To know that one's friend has been debauched by one's headmaster is truly horrible; to know that he neither regrets nor resents this, as Bright made it clear he did not when I tried to impress upon him the need to break off the connection, is worse. In these circumstances the silence Bright imposed on me eventually became intolerable − how I hope you will not condemn me for breaking it at last.

I have now, in telling you the whole, cast my bread upon the waters − but I hope it will not return to me after many days, for I have to tell you that as Dr Onslow's former pupil I would find it impossible personally to take any action in this case should you think it necessary. This impossibility has, like my word given to Bright, kept me silent till now, and I do not think you will wonder at it. Mr Mildmay, however, insists it is not for me but for you as my parent to do what you will, sir, and it is in obedience to his instructions that I am writing to you and awaiting your decision. I expect I ought to tell you that it is Mr Mildmay's opinion that Dr Onslow ought to be forced to resign his post at Charton, on the grounds that he is clearly not a man fit to have charge of young boys, despite his notable achievements. I do not know whether you will agree with this view, but those achievements, I must now tell you, are less great at least in the moral sphere than report makes them out to be.

The moral condition of Charton is in fact very bad. Sensual vice of all kinds flourishes there wholly unchecked, and I cannot but believe that this is a result of the Headmaster's being unable to control his own passions. From him, after all, stems all authority, all power to correct. The other masters, and the monitors, take their tone from him, and the result is that young boys on their arrival at Charton are at the very least forced to witness hideous scenes of immorality, at worst seduced by older boys and referred to thereafter as 'bitches', and called by female names.

You have no need, my dear Father, to fear for me. I succeeded in resisting all attempts to corrupt me, and have paradoxically been given, by my unfortunate education, a lifelong horror of that kind of vice and a love of all that is pure, all who are pure. It would have been best no doubt had I learnt to love what is good by having it placed before me in school, instead of through the natural revulsion I felt for its opposite, for perhaps I cannot be said to have emerged scatheless from Charton. Since going there, and more especially since learning that Dr Onslow is himself morally corrupt, I have become more cynical than I expect you would like me to be. It seems to me that there is very little good in this world, where an ordained clergyman can administer communion to his pupils one day and debauch them the next. How much I wonder whether Dr Onslow is ever troubled in his conscience – I doubt it very much.

You may wonder, sir, why I did not tell you of the vile acts I witnessed at Charton while I was still there. The truth is that I feared you would not believe me, and that I could not have borne. It seemed to me that I had nothing to do but endure.

Dear Father, I have suffered very much over this whole affair, and I now implore you not to seek to involve me yet more closely in it, or even to talk to me about it when I am back at home, whether or not you choose to do as Mr

Mildmay advises – I find it too painful, as I hope you will understand.

There is some possibility that our visit to Switzerland may be extended, in which case I shall not be back in England until the very end of August. Please write to me – not only about this, but with all your news, and Rose's and Aunt Chatty's too.

I remain your affectionate son
Christian

I hope you will not think it necessary to make a public scandal – I ask this for my friend Bright's sake, and the sake of all the others whom Dr Onslow may have corrupted.

Including me, thought Christian as he read through his letter – and folded it, and sealed it, and walked the four miles down to Interlaken to post it.

On his way back, Christian began to shiver in the mountain breeze, for in his eagerness to be rid of his letter he had gone out too thinly clad. His mind became full of images of his father's turning round and telling him, in a voice full of disgust, that he had burnt the evidence against Onslow, and that no son of his ought under any circumstances to break a bond of silence and then seek to escape the consequences. By the time he reached the chalet, Christian was certain that this was what his father would do, and he went up to his bedroom and wept: for remorse, for resentment, and for Jemmy who was pure.

━━━

The letter from Christian arrived at Poplar House five days after it was posted, on July 14th, and was handed to Anstey-Ward by Rose. He was out in the garden at the time, delicately removing encrusted dirt from the indentations of a fossilised trilobite, and was not much pleased by the interruption.

'A letter from Christian, Father. I thought you might like to have it immediately, and Mary Jane was afraid to disturb you.'

'Very well, my dear, put it down there.'

83

His imagination was busy with a picture of himself proving to the satisfaction of the Geological Society that the stratum of Welsh rock in which he found the trilobite had been assigned to the wrong period. Only when he acknowledged that he was unlikely ever to find conclusive evidence for something so improbable did he lay the fossil aside, resettle his spectacles on his nose and open the letter. He had been wanting to hear from Christian for some time, for he was anxious about the state of his lungs, and hoped that the Alpine air had done them good. Christian's mother had died of consumption.

Anstey-Ward read Christian's letter through twice, slowly and steadily, and then examined the enclosed notes, the evidence. At last he laid the papers down and sat quite still. His mind was chiefly occupied not with Onslow, but with his son – who, he thought, having been exposed to abomination, would never make some girl a good husband one day. Anstey-Ward had begun to suspect this some time ago, but now he knew it with absolute certainty, and he blamed not only Onslow but himself.

He had always known that Christian did not much like Charton, but till now he had never known why. He had never asked questions, and had therefore, he supposed, given his son the impression that his own father would not listen to him, still less believe him, if he told the truth. Christian had not trusted him. Aged fourteen, he had never thought to save himself by coming into his father's library and explaining precisely why he hated school. They had been less close and less confident even than he thought – and they never would be close now. Christian made it very clear that closeness and confidence were not what he wanted in the future, that even his father's advice would not be welcome.

The boy had only ever asked to be taken away from school in a casual and tentative murmur. He had seemed to accept that it was right for him to go to Charton, where, so his father thought, he was protected from the rougher side of school life by the intellectual excellence which quickly raised him in the hierarchy. Boys at Charton did not sleep in dormitories but in rooms for two or three at most, and Anstey-Ward had supposed this guaranteed a certain level of civilised conduct. It was true that he had been at Charton himself for two half-years when he was sixteen, and had seen some bad things, but that had been in 1824. Dr Onslow was said to have put a stop to all the old abuses. Anstey-Ward's chief concern when he sent Christian to the school had been the possibility that his son would learn to be too earnest in religion, and become a prig.

As he remembered this, Anstey-Ward's eyes fell on Christian's mention of Onslow's administering communion to his boys prior to debauching them, and he drew in a long, sharp breath.

He had lost his own religious faith painlessly as a young man, thanks chiefly to philosophy, not geology, but he had never been strongly anti-religious – if only because such attitudes were for men of the lower classes who read Tom Paine. It was a decade or more since educated Christians had commonly believed in the literal truth of the first chapters of Genesis, and if that belief were abandoned Anstey-Ward had no serious quarrel with them. He disliked only those who objected noisily to men who were freethinkers, like himself.

Anstey-Ward accepted without question the morality of charity, patience, forgiveness, continence, and called it Christian without a thought, for he tended to associate monstrous cruelties, abuses and hypocrisies only with the Catholic church, not with most forms of Protestantism, and certainly not with the reformed Church of England. He expected the clergy to conform to his high opinion of their morals at all times: he was therefore as shocked by his son's revelation of Dr Onslow's true character as the most naively devout of Christians would have been – and his feelings were unmixed with any sense of excitement, or of the dreadful grandeur of notable sin.

14

On July 17th, Dr and Mrs Onslow were entertaining five boys to breakfast between first and second school. They did this once a week in term-time, and thus saw every boy at Charton informally at least once a year. The boys invited were of mixed ages, for though Louisa had at first suggested that the younger ones would be less painfully shy without their seniors, this had been discovered not to be the case. Nothing could induce eleven or twelve-year-olds to make conversation with the headmaster, though some of them felt able to talk to his wife, and if no older boys had been present breakfast would have been almost entirely silent. As it was, the young ones ate as much of the food provided by Louisa as they could manage, while their elders answered Dr Onslow's questions, and in their turn asked him gravely about current events, or complimented his wife on the elegance of the breakfast-room.

'So now I hear you are in the Eleven, Browning,' said Onslow to a fifth-former. 'You must be very pleased.'

'Yes, sir.'

Wishing to rouse him, Onslow went on: 'I cannot be surprised at it. And yet I sometimes think too much is made of games at this school. Is it really necessary to put on white trousers before kicking a ball in a muddy field? Last time I happened to pass the football field I saw that quite half the players were wearing striped jerseys in addition – I suppose they were introduced by the last captain of football, what was his name?'

'Tillotson, sir.'

'Tillotson, so it was, as in the Sermons which are no

86

longer read . . . Yes, he seemed to think football a sacred cause rather than a recreation, I remember him well.'

'Would you like it best, sir, if we played no games at all?' said another boy boldly.

'Let me express it this way, Johnson: I approve of physical exercise, and I had rather cricket and football were played than hare-and-hounds.' Hare-and-hounds was the preferred game of many boys during the Easter term: Onslow had tried to abolish it because it led to trouble with local farmers, but he had not been entirely successful.

'Oh, quite so, sir!'

Onslow smiled at him; he had an unusually charming smile when he was neither mocking nor being sarcastic.

'At my brother's school football is forbidden entirely,' said Browning, swallowing a piece of muffin. 'The headmaster thinks it is not a gentleman's game. But he allows cricket.'

'Football has been played here for so long that if I were to dare say I agreed with him, which I do not altogether, the Sixth would demand my resignation,' said Onslow. 'Is that not so, Caldecott?'

'Oh yes, sir, certainly we would!' said the sixth-former, who had been talking to Louisa about the summer exhibition at the Royal Academy.

'Winthrop, won't you have a little more coffee? And another devilled kidney?' said Louisa to one of the younger boys. 'And you too, Talbot, of course.'

'Oh yes please, Mrs Onslow ma'am!'

Talbot and Winthrop were twelve years old. When Louisa first came to Charton, the youngest boys in the school were eight and nine, but now Onslow discouraged parents from sending him children under eleven. He thought very young boys were best off as private pupils, and Louisa was sorry for it, for she liked children, though she knew that Onslow was probably right. The little ones had been more prone than others to die when they were ill, not only of cholera and typhoid and scarlatina but of measles and putrid sore throat, to which the older boys seemed more immune.

Onslow glanced swiftly at the clock on the mantelpiece, and saw that second school would begin in ten minutes. As soon as one of the boys made a movement which could be interpreted as preparatory to leaving, he said:

'Must you go? Can't you stay?' He always dismissed those who came to breakfast with these words; it was a school legend that occasionally he muddled the formula, and said: 'Must you stay? Can't you go?'

Everyone except Louisa rose from the table as soon as the words were spoken. Thanks were said, compliments exchanged; then the headmaster and his wife were left alone together.

'It is a whole week till you will be obliged to endure it again, my dear,' said Louisa.

'Very true. Please hand me those letters I see on the sideboard, and the *Morning Post* – how glad I am to have a respite from boys' company, however brief! And yet I would not say that I dislike them.'

Onslow had no lessons till third school, for the Sixth would be occupied with mathematics for the next two hours. Dr Anstey-Ward had favoured Charton over other schools partly because Onslow insisted that mathematics be taught with something like seriousness. Three hours a week were devoted to it by every form, and to advertise the importance of his subject, the mathematics master had the right to wear a gown like the classical masters.

Two maids came in to clear away the remains of the boys' breakfast, leaving the Onslows with tea and toast. Onslow began to slit open his letters. When he was in a good humour, he would briefly describe any particularly interesting or foolish letter to his wife; when not, he would go straight to his study with them when he had finished eating.

'From Mrs Matlock – someone, unnamed for a wonder, has told her that it is now essential for prospective army officers to take a very difficult examination, she does not know what dear Lord Raglan and the dear Duke of Wellington would have said and is her Willie being properly prepared for it? This is the fourth letter I have had from her since April. The more I know of widows as parents,

88

the more I find myself reconsidering my objections as to suttee – how am I to tell her politely that her Willie is quite safe since we have not yet abolished purchase, and until that is done I have no intention of wasting school time in preparing for the army those who are too stupid for any other profession.'

'Tell her simply that he is so clever he will have no difficulty,' suggested Louisa.

'My dear, that would be a lie so big that even Mrs Matlock would know it for what it was, and I could not reconcile it with my conscience. I had best advise her to take him away.' He opened a second letter and glanced first at the signature, as he always did when he did not recognise the handwriting. 'H. A. Anstey-Ward – there was a boy called Anstey-Ward who left last year, I seem to remember.'

'It cannot be from him, Dr Onslow, his name was Christian,' said Louisa.

'Your memory is remarkable, my dear.'

Onslow proceeded to read the letter, which was very short.

Sir, it said, *certain documents have come into my possession, which inform me that, a year ago, you formed an illicit connection with one of your pupils, now no longer at Charton. I will not elaborate upon the documents' nature, but think it right to tell you that they show, conclusively, that you are a man entirely unfit for the position you now hold.*

I therefore demand that you resign the headmastership of Charton forthwith. If you refuse to do so, I shall have no hesitation in making a public example of you. I insist, also, that you refuse any high preferment which may be offered you upon your resignation. If you are unfit to have charge of young boys, you are likewise unfit to be a bishop or dean of the Church of England.

I remain, sir, your obedt. servt., H. A. Anstey-Ward.

Onslow sat completely motionless, holding the letter before him – then he forced himself to read it a second time. It was as though a great wave had crashed down upon his head. He felt much as he had done at the end of the great railway speculation of 1846, when he learnt that all the money he had inherited from his father had vanished in the crash, and he was liable for a part of the railway company's debts.

'Dr Onslow, what is wrong?'

Slowly he looked up at Louisa. His lips tried to move, but no sound came out.

'Tell me!'

'No,' he said at last. 'Nothing is wrong.'

'It's that letter you are holding. Please show it to me! You look as though you have seen a ghost.'

'No,' said Onslow again. The sight of Louisa's face and the sound of her voice dragged him back into the real world. Pushing his chair back, he went on almost normally: 'I promise you, my dear, there is no need for you to concern yourself. It is a – a comparatively trifling matter, merely something of a shock to me. But I need to go – to London immediately.' The idea of going to London, and thence to Salisbury, came into Onslow's head only as he spoke these words.

'George,' said Louisa, who called him that only on the most solemn occasions, 'please tell me what it is.'

The idea of doing this was so appalling that Onslow spoke sharply to her.

'I have told you that that is quite unnecessary. Please do not seek to make matters more difficult than they need be.'

'Very well!' said Louisa, setting down her tea-cup with unnecessary force.

'I am going to consult Bradshaw. I hope to be back by tonight, but I may be obliged to spend the night in town.'

'Is it money? Will you please only tell me that?'

'Yes – yes, it is money.' Onslow was not a skilful liar: Dr Arnold's training made it impossible for him to tell a direct falsehood without suffering greatly in his conscience.

'But it cannot be!' said Louisa, suddenly remembering who the letter was from.

'Louisa, leave me in peace!' Onslow went quickly out of

the room. The exchange with his wife had the effect of fully awakening his numb mind, and in his study, as he leafed through Bradshaw's railway guide, he found himself able to think.

He thrust emotion away. His concern was not to let himself dwell on the position in which he found himself, but simply to escape from it. He could do that, he thought, only by confronting Anstey-Ward and demanding to see the 'documents' – which he hoped would prove to be simply letters from Christian Anstey-Ward alleging that he had been the lover of a boy. The whole tone of the father's letter made it possible that they would turn out to be no more, and allegations of that kind would not constitute proof. Without proof, Anstey-Ward could not force him to resign. He would have no power to make a scandal – Onslow refused to think about the amount of damage mere rumour could do. He reminded himself that prejudice would be on the side of the Headmaster of Charton. Sober people would refuse to think ill of him, even though there might be degrading tittle-tattle in the clubs and drawing-rooms of London. It was a comforting picture.

Onslow acted with the utmost efficiency. First he found a suitable train. Next he rang the bell and told the servant who answered it to see that a small portmanteau was packed and the carriage was brought round; then he sat down at his desk and wrote a note to Mr Grey, the second master, to say that he was called away on urgent business, and to ask him to make provision for the Sixth.

While he was in the middle of doing this, the door opened. It was his wife, and glancing at her in profound irritation, he thought she was looking almost old.

'George,' said Louisa, closing the door, 'is it blackmail?'

He turned round in his chair, and stared at her.

'*Blackmail*? What in the world are you talking about, Louisa?'

'I know you have received extremely bad news.'

Onslow laid down his pen and said, having only just realised that blackmail might indeed have been a real possibility:

'I will no longer conceal that from you, since you seem to be so unnaturally percipient. But I assure you it is not blackmail. What a lurid imagination you have; this is what comes of reading novels from the circulating library. Pray, about what could I be blackmailed? Have you decided of what crime I am guilty?' His face was flushed.

'A boy,' said Louisa.

In the silence, the clock struck ten.

15

Louisa watched her husband's face and then went on in a great hurry, as though she were confessing to a grave misdeed.

'You must not be so surprised that I know about your feelings for some of the boys. After all, I am your wife, and it is not so odd that over the years I should have guessed, discovered.' Onslow continued to stare and say nothing. 'Oh, dear, I wish I had never told you! I would never have done so were it not that I was almost sure. I thought it would relieve you a little of care if you only knew it was not essential to make sure everything was concealed from me. *Is* it blackmail?'

'No,' said Onslow at last.

'What is it?' She paused. 'Or would you rather know first how I know?'

'Yes,' he replied, realising that by his dreadful silence he had already revealed that she was right in her suspicions, approximately right. It would be useless to pretend he thought her mad.

'It was four or five years ago,' said Louisa, steadily refusing to let her eyes fall to the floor. 'I was in the drawing-room, fetching some wools from behind the screen, and you came in with a boy only for a moment. I heard a very brief exchange, but it was enough.' In a voice rough with anxiety, Onslow had asked the boy for a kiss. After that, Louisa had kept her eyes open, and sorted out her thoughts.

Onslow said now furiously: 'And you neither screamed nor fainted? I must be infinitely obliged to you!' He thought he had never known what shame was till this moment.

'No, of course not. It was a surprise, but – but it is such an unusual failing, and so small in comparison with other husbands. Loose women, and strong drink – I am not altogether ignorant of the world, you know, Dr Onslow.'

Onslow snapped a pencil in two, and threw the pieces down.

'So I must receive not one but two blows this morning. It is insufferable. How dared you not tell me before this?'

Louisa remained calm. 'I knew it was something about which you would not want me to know. I could hear it in your voice when you spoke to that boy. As I said, I never would have told you – '

'Will you please say no more!'

'May I not ask now what was in that letter?'

There was a pause. Then Onslow drew in his breath and said, less harshly but more awkwardly than he had spoken before:

'He says I am, I must – oh, you may as well read it for yourself.' He took the letter out of his inside pocket, and Louisa came over to take it from his hand. She went to read it on the sofa, leaving him to his thoughts.

Desperately Onslow wondered whether he ought to probe into his wife's extraordinary mind, or whether he ought rather simply accept the new, adult, amoral person whom she had revealed herself to be – the dangerous creature who thought his failing small. It was intolerable that Louisa should be such a person, for he expected his wife to have the highest moral standards as well as to be forever childlike. Yet it was, after a fashion, comforting to think that he was not entirely alone, neither physically nor mentally alone, as Anstey-Ward would doubtless wish him to be in the obscurity to which he had condemned him.

Before Louisa had finished reading the letter, a servant came in to tell Onslow that his portmanteau was packed and the carriage would soon be at the door. Onslow, who had quite forgotten his plans for leaving immediately, stared uncomprehendingly at the man before he said:

'Tell them to wait.' There was no way, now, he could

make efficient decisions, as he had done before Louisa came in.

As soon as the servant was gone, Louisa folded Anstey-Ward's letter and said:

'He writes almost as though he had some private grudge against you, and has been longing for just such an opportunity to vent his spleen.'

'Do you think so? I am sure you are a judge, Mrs Onslow.'

'He is very hard. I cannot believe that he honestly means to wreck your whole life.'

'Precisely.'

'But I am glad that at least it is not blackmail.'

'Are you? Would that not be preferable?'

'No, whatever are you thinking of? To be always unsafe, always wretched – this is at least *clean*.' Then came the question Onslow was dreading. 'What are these documents, Dr Onslow? You did not write to this boy, did you? How can such letters have come into this man's possession, if you did?'

After a moment he said:

'I am very sure that the documents to which he refers are no such thing. If they were, he would have been more specific. As it is, he hopes pompously to overawe me, trusting to my guilty conscience.'

'But you did write – incriminating letters?'

'Louisa,' said Onslow, turning round to face her, 'are you indeed not very much shocked? Do you not think I am very wicked?'

She opened her eyes wide. 'No, I think you foolish.'

'Foolish!' It was a word and a thing he hated. He thought of how for ten years, ever since he first gave way to temptation, he had supposed that only his own confession could make others aware. His whole reliance had been on the boyish code of silence, and even now, he could not acknowledge that his disgrace was inevitable, only because someone had discovered his private business without his permission.

'I want to know whether you wrote letters to a boy.'

'That is my own affair,' he said, turning briefly back to the papers on his desk.

'Did you tell him to burn them?'

'Yes!'

'And you are certain he did so?'

'I have had enough of this inquisition. You forget yourself.'

'Then what are these documents, Dr Onslow?'

Turning to face her again, Onslow coldly explained his belief that they were mere allegations made by Anstey-Ward's son, and as he did so, he was forced to draw the obvious conclusion that another boy had told Christian Anstey-Ward – he had not thought of that before. Quickly he decided that Arthur Bright would never have told. Christian Anstey-Ward must therefore have discovered his previous love-affair, with a boy called Hallam, which had ended in 1856.

'How can you be so incredibly calm?' he asked his wife, having watched her look only mildly disturbed throughout his explanation.

'Where would be the use of my flying into hysterics?'

'You are a cold-hearted woman, Louisa,' said Onslow, who had always valued Louisa because she was immune to tantrums and hysterics. 'And you have a secretive disposition.'

'I am not, and I have not.' For the first time, she looked both angry and unhappy. 'It is unjust. You have every reason to be grateful to me.'

'I must acknowledge it. Louisa . . .' He did not know what to say next. Then suddenly, emotion rushed through him like a great jet of water: Louisa had never looked more like her brother than at that moment, and Onslow was able to think of her not as amoral, but as infinitely forgiving. 'Louisa, before God, I know what a terrible injury I have done you. Believe me, the thought that if I am ruined you must be ruined too is the worst of all, the worst punishment I shall have to suffer!'

'Oh, Dr Onslow, don't talk in that style!'

'It is true.'

There was a long and awkward pause. Then Louisa said:

'What are we going to do?'

Onslow, in obedience to his dying emotional impulse, went over to sit beside her. He took one of her hands in his and removed the letter from the other, and, gently pushing her skirt aside, he said:

'I am going down to Wiltshire to see him, to talk to him. That is all I can do.' The alternative was to submit in silence, but Onslow did not consider doing that for a moment. 'I need to see whatever it is he has in his possession.'

'Today?'

'Yes, today.'

'Dr Onslow, you cannot. To arrive so precipitately would be to give the impression that you know yourself to be – to be justly accused.'

He flushed. 'Then pray what do you suggest I do?'

'I think we ought to go together to see him. Not today, but later.'

'No!'

'I want to come with you.'

'I refuse to permit it.'

'Why?'

'Because I presume you have some notion of wheedling him into a less vengeful frame of mind, should it be necessary, and my pride will not stomach it.' Onslow had swung back from thinking his wife an angel to thinking her a meddlesome woman and indifferent to sin.

'Your pride,' said Louisa. 'Very well. I will accompany you only to – to lend you silent support.'

'No, Louisa.'

'But I want to come so much. George, I cannot bear to be left out, to be kept waiting here alone. Surely, in a sense, you owe it to me?'

'No.'

Louisa got up from the sofa and said:

'Only a moment ago you were almost beside yourself at the thought of what you called the injury you have done me. I do not think it is so great an injury in itself, but by your – your folly, you have placed yourself in a position where I too am in danger of being ruined. As you said.'

'And so?' said Onslow angrily.

'I think you owe it to me to grant my wish in this matter.'

'Why do you wish to come?'

'To – to be a comfort to you if I can, to be a part of things. But I will own that although I have no intention of – of begging Dr Anstey-Ward to be kinder to you, I hope my presence will remind him that you have a wife whose life must needs be spoilt with yours, if he holds by his intention.'

'I see,' said Onslow, thinking of how most men found Louisa very charming. He was once more back to thinking of her as a perfect Christian like her brother. By failing to be horrified, by forgiving him, she had raised herself to a moral level immeasurably high above his own – he was beginning to agree that in the circumstances he, the author of her possible ruin, had no choice but to grant her wish.

Louisa, glancing at him quickly, saw that he was on the point of giving in. Turning to face the window, she sucked in her lips to control a smile. Her husband must never guess that to be in danger excited her as much as it distressed her, and that she was very sure she could prevent Anstey-Ward from abiding by his plan.

'Very well,' said Onslow. 'You may come with me. But I leave today.'

'Dr Onslow, do but consider. It will look so odd if we arrive without warning – I am thinking partly of the Anstey-Ward ladies, I remember Christian Anstey-Ward had seven elder sisters. Truly, I think you ought to send a telegraphic message. We could go down tomorrow, leaving early, if you are not willing to leave it till next week.'

'Tomorrow is a Sunday, Louisa.'

'Oh, so it is. Well, in that case we must wait until Monday – it would be fatal for you, a clergyman, to travel on a Sunday – it would reveal all your anxiety.'

'Very well, very well, we shall go on Monday, together. I put myself in your hands.'

In this way, Onslow atoned for the injury he had done his wife.

98

16

Soon after he put his letter in the post-bag and saw it taken away, Anstey-Ward began to suffer certain qualms of conscience. He did not believe he had done the wrong thing, but he wished another man could have been called on to do the right thing: a man whose own conduct was and always had been exemplary. His was not. He could not accuse himself of sins of the flesh, because such sins had never tempted him, and he could not understand why other men did not do as nature and reason demanded – beget a few children and then withdraw into the life of the mind. But though he could neither understand nor empathise with Onslow's passion, Anstey-Ward was forced to empathise with his hypocrisy, the way in which he shamelessly pretended to be what he was not. He had himself once been a hypocrite.

His hypocrisy consisted of having gone to church regularly, and contributed to Christian missions, and wholly hidden his unbelief, in the days when he had been obliged to earn his living. The memory of his behaviour towards one lucrative old lady made him squirm inwardly whenever he thought of it. He had tutted with her over Dr Buckland's abandonment of belief in a universal deluge, assured her that his own researches had not led him to doubt Scripture, and let several pints of her blood over the years only to please her, though he held the outdated treatment to be both superstitious and dangerous. And when a clergyman told him that to use anaesthesia was to thwart God's purpose, he had argued against him not from reason and humanity, but by reminding him that God put Adam to sleep before taking out his rib.

Anstey-Ward's conscience was as active as any Christian's. Before Onslow's telegram arrived, he came near to persuading himself that it was wrong for him to judge the man's conduct, no matter how badly his son's innocence had been damaged. To force him to resign was to do his duty by the boys of Charton, but to forbid him to accept high preferment was to make a judgement from on high, where he had no right to be.

But Onslow's cool telegram, saying merely *Mrs Onslow and I arriving Monday afternoon*, threw Anstey-Ward back into thinking that in spite of all he had done the right thing. It took him wholly by surprise, for it had not occurred to him that Onslow would seek to confront him, to challenge him and argue, as he could only assume was now his intention. He had supposed that a proud, reserved cleric, which he judged Onslow to be, would never acknowledge such a communication as he had made. He had expected him simply to obey its commands in silence, pretending all the while to his acquaintance that there was nothing amiss. The whole indecent business would be covered up, forgotten.

Yet even so, both before and after Onslow's telegram came, Anstey-Ward indulged in imaginary and fantastic conversations with his adversary. In these, Onslow begged to be spared. Anstey-Ward then told him that no, he could not be spared, that indeed he ought to be held up publicly as an example of wickedness and cynical corruption amongst those whose business it was to set an example. Next he expatiated not only on the vice of hypocrisy, but on the role played by sexual irregularities in the decay of great nations such as Imperial Rome: he told Onslow that orgies and decadence would destroy England as surely as they had the great empire of antiquity, and went on to say that it was the duty of humanity to copy the beasts, who, as nature demanded, copulated only for offspring.

When he thought of the kind of conversation he and Onslow were likely to have in reality, Anstey-Ward felt suffocated with embarrassment. The idea of showing Onslow the letters was horrible, for it made the whole

100

situation too real, and it made him seem like a blackmailer. But he was determined not to be bullied into mildness by a man accustomed to frightening schoolboys, and he kept up his courage by thinking of how greatly Onslow had offended, how monstrously he had deceived the world, far more monstrously than he had done himself. His mind went round and round the question as he waited and waited, on July 19th, for Onslow and Louisa to arrive.

'Whatever can be keeping them?' said Chatty.

'I daresay they must have missed their train,' he replied. It was six o'clock, and they had just finished their dinner. The Onslows had been expected at four.

'Do you suppose they will come today at all, if that is so?'

'I don't know, Chatty,' said Anstey-Ward.

'I wish I knew what urgent business you can have with Dr Onslow. And why, in that case, he is bringing his wife with him.'

'I expect they are going on to visit friends in this neighbourhood.'

Anstey-Ward found it hard to believe Onslow would be quite so cold-blooded as that, but his wife's coming seemed to indicate it. It did not occur to him that Louisa was no innocent, and knew the reason for her husband's visiting him.

'Henry, if they do come later today, I think we ought to offer them beds for the night,' said Chatty. 'Unless of course they are going straight on to their friends, as you suggested.'

'For the night?'

'It would be only civil.'

'Very well,' said Anstey-Ward slowly. He had told Chatty that his business with Onslow was urgent, but had dropped no hint that it was exceedingly unpleasant, and he felt that to brush her suggestion aside in disgust would be to put disagreeable notions into her woman's head.

Onslow was furious at having missed the train, which he maintained had left Waterloo before the time advertised by the company. Louisa did not agree with him, but did not contradict him. She wished he were not so nervous.

In the crawling, cheap parliamentary train, which they had been obliged to take instead of the express, they both read books: Louisa a French novel and Onslow Horace's *Satires*. But when the old gentleman who had been sharing their carriage got out at Basingstoke, they gradually ceased to concentrate on their reading matter, and began to think and worry. They might have talked, but Onslow at least did not wish to, and Louisa could see it.

She thought how fortunate she was in that her husband did not humiliate her and disgrace his cloth by running after other women – she had reminded herself of this several times since she discovered his strange passion for boys. Louisa wondered whether there were many other men who shared his taste, for she could not know. No book she had ever been allowed to read described the love of men for boys. No one had ever mentioned it to her, and told her what to think, and thus she had drawn her own conclusion that it was eccentric and uncomfortable, rather than immoral. Only certain words of St Paul's, and Onslow's hushed anxious voice in the drawing-room five years ago, had told her that here was something wrong – but quite why it was so very wrong, she did not understand.

Louisa failed to imagine sodomy. She imagined embraces only one degree removed from those indulged in openly by men who loved each other, like Onslow and Primrose, who enfolded each other warmly on meeting and parting – she saw cuddles and kisses, and pattings of the virile member. Thus she thought Anstey-Ward utterly unreasonable, and was sure that she would be able to make him see reason, if Onslow was unsuccessful. Unlike her husband, she did not try to make herself believe that the 'documents' would turn out to be mere unsubstantiated libel: her confidence was entirely rooted in the fact that Anstey-Ward was making himself ridiculous, and as she did not doubt, could be brought by subtle means to see it.

102

Onslow, frowning at the carriage window, dared no longer cherish the hope that the evidence against him would amount to very little. His dread was that Arthur Bright had been careless with his letters, and allowed one to find its way into Christian Anstey-Ward's hands. The more he thought about it, the more likely it seemed. Onslow wondered what crazy impulse had driven him to abandon the discretion of years, and write letters without even making quite sure that his lover understood the importance of burning them. By doing so, unless he could save himself at the last moment, he had at last fulfilled his mother's frequently reiterated prophecy that he would come to a bad end.

He glanced at Louisa, and saw that she was watching him. He turned away again, but Louisa did not let her eyes fall. The desire to talk was welling up in her, irresistible as a wish to sneeze. She fidgeted, and opened her novel, knowing that Onslow would reject her, but in the end she could resist no longer, and said:

'Dr Onslow – what is it draws you to boys?'

He looked at her as though she were a pupil guilty of some unbelievable impertinence, but after a moment his eyes became less fierce, and he said stiffly:

'I do not know, Louisa. I wish I did. Forgive me, but I cannot talk about it.'

'No,' said Louisa, and looked down, biting her lip to keep back words. Her hands were shaking as they clutched her book.

It was true that he did not know, for he had always avoided thinking about his passion except in his most conscience-stricken moments, when a sense of guilt prevented him from examining the matter clearly. Now he tried to do so, but he merely succeeded in visualising his four boy lovers – three of them blended into one face, but Bright remained alone. The pleasure to be had from their beauty was as keen and as nasty as the pain to be had from a birch.

A birch. Onslow shifted in his seat as he blamed his falling into sin on his headmaster's duty of flogging boys.

He thought if it were not for that, he would never have given way to desire, never have known he desired – but it was not that he enjoyed inflicting pain, as some did. He wanted to inflict pleasure more than anything else in the world.

He thought once more of his lovers. When lusting, he demanded vigorous young animals, boys with a distinct flavour, he told himself, of evil – every one of his boys had been pagan Bacchus to him while he lasted. He wanted a strong musky smell and wild curling hair, eyes gleaming with knowledge, no taint of purity. To drink at the fountain of such boys was to drink the wine of wickedness, eat the delicious forbidden. It was to defy the memories of his mother and even of Dr Arnold. In this lay the sin, thought Onslow: not lust but rebellion, a form of pride. But that was no concern of Dr Anstey-Ward's.

At last, at nearly seven o'clock, the train drew into Salisbury. The Onslows began to talk again.

'Shall we go straight to Dr Anstey-Ward?' said Louisa, re-tying the strings of her bonnet.

'No, I mean to dine first. We have eaten nothing since this morning, and I will scarcely be fit to handle him if I am nearly faint with hunger. We shall go to an hotel.'

'Very well. I hope they will be able to give us a room for the night.'

'If not, I do not intend to waste time searching all Salisbury. We must go straight to Dr Anstey-Ward and look for one when we come back.'

'Dr Onslow, no hotel will think us respectable if we arrive at nearly midnight, and with so little luggage.'

'Nonsense, Louisa. You talk as though we were a pair of travelling actors. A clergyman is always respectable,' he said, and smiled faintly.

17

The Salisbury Hotel was not able to supply the Onslows
with a bed for the night as well as with dinner, but it
furnished them with a chaise, and they set out for Poplar
House at a quarter to nine. When they arrived, it was
almost dark, and they could see only the yellow gleam of
lighted windows, and the square black outline of the house
against a sapphire-coloured sky.

In the drawing-room, Anstey-Ward heard the crunch of
carriage wheels on the gravel outside. He got up and looked
out of the window, and saw Onslow helping his wife out of
the carriage. Louisa's skirt was dragged up at the back in
the process, and he had a glimpse of her legs.

'It's they,' he said to his sister.

'Arriving at this hour! I wonder they could not leave it
till morning, it surely cannot be so urgent as all that.'

On the doorstep, Onslow said to Louisa:

'Can you not remember what he is like to look at? I
suppose I must have met him at some point, but I cannot
recall him.'

'No, I cannot precisely, but I have some idea that he is a
cadaverous-looking man – very tall and thin, and ascetic
looking.'

'How very appropriate.'

They rang the bell, and it was answered. After taking
their cards through, the parlour-maid showed them into
the big, ugly drawing-room, where they at last set eyes on
Anstey-Ward. His far from cadaverous appearance was
initially a surprise to them both, but on seeing him, they
remembered having met him once before. Onslow thought

105

that he looked for all the world like a rotund paterfamilias in a *Punch* cartoon as he bore down upon them smiling, with an outstretched hand.

'Dr Onslow, how very glad I am to see you – and you too, of course, Mrs Onslow. How good of you to come all this way so late!'

'I am sorry,' said Onslow, taken aback, 'but owing to the press of traffic in London we missed the train we intended to catch.'

'A great nuisance, but it does not signify. Now, you must allow me to make you known to my sister, Miss Anstey-Ward.'

Anstey-Ward beamed down at them as he indicated his sister. Onslow, responding, was displeased to see that the woman was a good deal taller than he was, like Anstey-Ward himself. He could only be glad that there was no sign of the seven young ladies whom Louisa had warned him to expect – he saw his wife looking discreetly round her as though she thought they would come out from behind the curtains.

Chatty smiled as she shook hands with the Onslows. Though she had complained about their coming so late, she was well pleased to be entertaining such a distinguished clergyman. She said:

'I have been meaning to buy your latest volume of sermons, Dr Onslow – I wish I had it with me, and then you might have signed it for me.'

'I should have been delighted to do so.'

'Yes, it's a thousand pities you haven't yet bought it, Chatty,' said Anstey-Ward.

Onslow supposed Anstey-Ward was being so friendly for the sake of his sister's innocence. It was a surprisingly great relief to him to think she was ignorant.

'My brother and I are hoping you will stay to supper, and discuss your business afterwards,' said Chatty, and her brother said:

'We are indeed! We shall be quite offended if you do not.'

Chatty wondered why Anstey-Ward was being quite so

affable: it was not his way to be so even with his close friends. Perhaps, she thought, he owed Onslow money.

'We shall be sitting down to supper very soon now,' she said.

'Oh, how badly we have timed our visit!' said Louisa, who, like Onslow, guessed that Chatty knew nothing of what was toward.

'Not at all, ma'am,' said Anstey-Ward, acting as much for her benefit as for Chatty's. 'Nothing can be easier, if you will but agree to sup with us. And then Dr Onslow and I can go to my library. Eh, Dr Onslow?'

'Exactly so, Dr Anstey-Ward!' said Onslow, and without too much difficulty, he smiled. It was beginning to seem as though this really were a social visit.

'And we are also hoping,' Chatty went on, 'that you will agree to stop the night with us, unless perhaps you are going on to stay with friends. Do not think me inquisitive!'

'Oh, what a kind invitation!' said Louisa. 'But – '

'My dear Miss Anstey-Ward, we could not possibly put you to so much trouble,' said Onslow.

'It will be no trouble at all to either of us,' said Anstey-Ward, even though he wished his sister were not quite so hospitable.

'But I am sure we will find an hotel in Salisbury.' Onslow spoke in the voice of one willing to be persuaded, as Miss Anstey-Ward would like him to be.

'Oh, you cannot like to set out again so late, and hotel beds are never to be relied upon. Why, when I last stayed in an hotel, it was one of the very best in Brighton, yet for all that the sheets were not aired properly. I caught a nasty chill.'

'How very unpleasant!' said Louisa.

'If you do stop, you and I will have tomorrow morning, as well as tonight, Dr Onslow,' said Anstey-Ward. For a moment, the atmosphere was spoilt. 'Now, do pray stop with us! We shall be honoured,' he hastened to add.

'Very well, since you are so good, I think we shall be delighted to accept your invitation,' said Onslow. 'As Miss Anstey-Ward has said, an hotel bed is not something to be joyfully anticipated. My dear, are you agreeable?'

107

'Certainly I am, Dr Onslow.'

Louisa had been looking at the drawing-room table, and Onslow, following her gaze, saw that on it there rested a pile of tracts referring in large letters to Christ as the Lamb and the Redeemer. He concluded that Miss Anstey-Ward was a narrow Evangelical, as his mother had been, and that Anstey-Ward was so too – he wished he had not been swept into accepting the invitation to stay.

Anstey-Ward thought that unless Onslow insisted on talking about what had brought him down to Wiltshire tonight, he would avoid mentioning it until the morning, just before Onslow was about to leave the house. He felt that having been so welcoming, he could not turn round and talk about what was vile the moment the women left them alone, and then show Onslow to bed as though all were as it should be. The comedy must continue.

Thinking this, he smiled at Louisa, whose smallness moved him. With her great eyes, slender figure and broad cheekbones, she reminded him very much of his late wife, Renée, so much so that he wondered whether they could be related. He doubted it, for Renée had been the child of a ne'er-do-well writer, while as he knew, Mrs Onslow came from one of the foremost clerical families in England, and was a bishop's daughter. But despite the unlikelihood of their being kinswomen, he found himself thinking of Louisa as a kind of connection, someone for whom he was to some extent responsible.

'Now, you'll be wanting to take off your hats and coats,' he said, and Onslow noticed that both his voice and his choice of words were slightly vulgar.

The Onslows were shown upstairs to a cold bedroom, and then, having tidied themselves, they came down again. On entering the drawing-room for the second time, Louisa noticed a series of photographs on one wall, and indicating one of them she said:

'Is that not your son, Dr Anstey-Ward?'

'Yes, that's Christian – taken by his sister, who is staying with our cousins in London just at present. She's a fine photographer.'

'I am sorry we shall not meet her,' said Onslow. 'How well I remember your son, sir!' In fact, he could only just remember the boy when his photograph was pointed out to him. It showed Christian staring into space, trying to look inspired and soulful. Onslow supposed he was no doubt wishing to live up to his clothes: he was wearing the turned-down collar and loose necktie favoured by those with bohemian pretensions, and banned at Charton. Looking in the photograph's direction, he said:

'And is he now enjoying Cambridge?'

'He's at Oxford,' said Anstey-Ward, 'and liking it very well.'

'I am sure he must do well, he was an excellent pupil.' Onslow could remember nothing about Christian's school-work, but he did remember that the boy had spent two years under him in the Sixth, having risen into his form at a fairly early age. He remembered his tense, anxious face at the front of the class.

'Was he?' said Chatty. 'I've always found him sadly shatterbrained. Bookish, of course, but shatterbrained.'

'Oh, no. A naturally bookish boy, as you say, and a very fair scholar,' said Onslow. 'I wonder why I was so sure he had gone to Cambridge, not Oxford? My memory is not what it was!'

There was a slight pause, and Louisa was on the point of making a remark, but Chatty spoke first.

'What admirable changes you have wrought at Charton, Dr Onslow! I am sure my brother has often said that the school now is not at all what it was in his day.'

'I wouldn't have sent Christian had I not thought it very different,' said Anstey-Ward calmly.

'You were at Charton yourself, sir?' said Onslow, a little surprised.

'For a year only, when I was sixteen. Under Dr Thorneycroft.'

'Dr Thorneycroft was a wicked old tyrant, was he not, Henry?' said Chatty. 'Has he not that reputation, Dr Onslow?'

Onslow smiled. 'Madam, it would scarcely become me to

agree with you about my distinguished predecessor. Shall I say he was not a very effective tyrant?'

'I think that if I had been born a man I would have liked to become a schoolmaster. You, for instance, have done so much, and for so many!' she said.

'Indeed he has,' said Anstey-Ward. 'Mrs Onslow, won't you come a little nearer the fire? And you too, sir. Very cold for the time of year, ain't it?'

'It certainly is,' said Chatty. 'But I shall have a fire kindled in your bedroom, Mrs Onslow, so you need not fear to freeze tonight.'

'Oh, how kind of you. What an agreeable luxury, a bedroom fire in July!'

'Tell me more of how your son goes on at Oxford, Dr Anstey-Ward,' said Onslow, then added: 'Were you yourself there, is that perhaps why you chose it for him rather than Cambridge?' He doubted very much that Anstey-Ward had been educated at Oxford.

'No indeed. I studied medicine in Edinburgh, not being a classical scholar by any manner of means. Christian takes after his mother's family, being literary.'

'Am I right in remembering that it was his ambition to be a poet, Dr Anstey-Ward?' said Louisa.

'Quite right, ma'am. I can see you take a great interest in all your husband's pupils!'

Louisa gave him a pretty smile, and he felt a desire to pat her little hand as it rested on the arm of her chair.

'I try, Dr Anstey-Ward – but nothing exceeds Dr Onslow's own interest in his pupils,' she said.

At that moment the parlourmaid came in, and announced that supper was served.

18

Anstey-Ward softly shut the heavy door of the library, and then he and Onslow were alone together at last. Onslow, breathing rapidly, felt two profound longings. The first was for a stiff brandy, and the second was for Anstey-Ward not to raise the subject of the 'documents'. All through supper, as he chatted politely, he had been impatient to have done with the charade – but now the moment had come, he felt quite differently. Like Anstey-Ward, he wanted to put important business off till the morning, till the daylight. He did not want to feel the lash of his power till then. And it seemed somehow impossible, or at least unsuitable, to abandon the friendly manner they had both maintained for so long. Onslow now felt he could not bear to acknowledge its falsity.

He was much surprised when brandy was offered him, for he had been certain that Anstey-Ward, as a rigid Evangelical, would not offer spirits to a clergyman.

'Or, if you prefer it, a little hot gin?' said Anstey-Ward. 'A very wholesome liquor in my opinion, when it is of good quality – none of your Old Tom three parts vitriol!'

'Thank you, no, brandy is just what I like.'

Anstey-Ward poured two brandies, while Onslow read the spines of the books in front of him in a tall glass-fronted case. Anstey-Ward's amiable remark about gin cheered him, for he was sure the man would not, having made it, propose to show him the 'documents'. He did not notice that Anstey-Ward's voice was very nervous; he could only think of the man as confident, secure.

When he was handed his glass, Onslow drank as much as

111

he could without giving Anstey-Ward the impression that he was firstly, unclerical, and secondly, afraid. As he drank, he continued to look at the books, not at his host. Their authors' names were for the most part wholly unfamiliar to him: Buffon, Cuvier, Agassiz, Lamarck, St Hilaire. He recognised only those of the English scientists Lyell, Sedgwick and Buckland, and was surprised, for it was unusual for an Evangelical to have intellectual interests of any kind. Evangelicals tended to hold that too much speculation about either religion or the world could only subvert the stern but emotional faith in which salvation lay. It was a creed which Onslow profoundly despised, for to him, intellect was the buttress of faith except when it was second-rate.

'I see you are looking at my books, Dr Onslow,' said Anstey-Ward, so accustomed to his part of affable host that even had he planned to abandon it he would have felt pompous and cruel in doing so. 'Are you yourself interested in the natural sciences?'

'Not so much as I dare say I ought to be. I believe the last scientific work I read was Dr Whewell's *On the Plurality of Worlds*.' It was almost the only scientific book he had ever read, and he had chosen to read it because it had been recommended to him as a work which demolished various materialistic speculations about the universe, and reasserted old ideas of the unity of the truth and the supernatural origins of the human mind and spirit.

'"A book meant to show that throughout all infinity, There's nothing so grand as the Master of Trinity",' quoted Anstey-Ward, placing the stopper on the brandy decanter. 'Did you admire it, Dr Onslow?'

'Indeed I did.'

'Now there I differ from you. I don't believe natural theology has any place in the modern world, and it seemed to me Dr Whewell's book was almost more a work of natural theology than of science.'

'You believe,' said Onslow, 'that the study of nature can and ought to be divorced from the study of its creator, its designer?'

112

'But I don't believe in its creator,' said Anstey-Ward, and his voice was suddenly very low and serious. It was extremely rarely he had a chance to talk about his views and beliefs, and he was delighted to have found a topic of conversation which would keep them away from the subject of the letters in his desk drawer, but which was not merely polite. 'I am a materialist, effectively an atheist, if that word does not shock you too much. Come, let us sit down!'

Onslow felt as though he had received a blow in the stomach. To him, the word 'atheist' meant a ragged, radical and violent working man, a revolutionary bent on destroying all the order and security and beauty in the world. It was a word with far more dreadful connotations than 'unbeliever', or even than 'infidel', and there was no one in his whole acquaintance who applied those words to himself. He had thought it was Low Church rectitude which made Anstey-Ward decide to bring him down, but now his conduct was far better explained. Anstey-Ward, bent on striking a blow against the Church, would be impervious to all considerations of mercy towards one who had repented. It was only astonishing that he had not decided to make a public spectacle of his Christian opponent.

'Pray sit down, Dr Onslow,' said Anstey-Ward, indicating a great wing-chair in which Onslow would be like a horse in blinkers, unable to see what was on either side of him, and forced to look ahead. Onslow, seating himself in it, managed to say:

'Am I to suppose it was your scientific researches turned you into an atheist? I have heard of such things happening.'

'Oh, no, I could not say that. It started when I was a child – I remember being punished for asking repeatedly who was Cain's wife.'

Onslow blinked. He too could remember being punished by his mother for asking exactly that – not repeatedly, but only once. 'Please tell me more,' he said.

'Well,' said Anstey-Ward, swinging the brandy in his glass, 'I was never much of a hand at my lessons, but as I grew up I went on asking questions of the like kind. And in the end I came to question the First Cause. I did not see that it was necessary to postulate a First Cause outside the universe, for why should the universe not be its own First Cause? God is not a necessary hypothesis. Do you know, it was a parson taught me that. He mentioned some old divine who said something, how was it – it is vain to do with more things what can be done with fewer.'

Onslow began to realise that Anstey-Ward was enjoying himself. For the first time, he felt active hatred of him, and wished he could think of some crushing but highly civilised remark. But Anstey-Ward, watching him all the time, went on uninterrupted.

'Still, though I say it was not my scientific studies caused my loss of faith, I am perfectly certain that one day science will disprove the existence of God,' he continued cheerfully. 'Two hundred years ago the Church was forced to accept that the earth moves. Now it is being gradually forced to accept that it was not created six thousand years ago.' He spoke with confident optimism, for he considered that given time and the advance of knowledge, all things could be proved or disproved. He looked forward not to an open and fluid intellectual universe, but to a dogmatic world in which the dogmas were true, instead of false. 'I take pleasure in being ahead of my time. I don't believe there will be such a thing as a Christian scientist to be found a hundred years from now.'

'The existence of God,' said Onslow, 'is not something which can be proved or disproved according to scientific notions of proof. It can only be known by faith.'

'Ay, in other words not known at all – but as for proof and disproof, we shall see,' said Anstey-Ward.

'In consequence,' said Onslow, pleased that Anstey-Ward had not followed his argument, 'there may well continue to be Christian scientists.'

'But it is already impossible for a man to be a good speculative scientist and a wholly orthodox believer so far at least as the Old Testament is concerned. Consider the fool poor Mr Gosse made of himself when he published his *Omphalos* – even some churchmen I could mention were embarrassed – I knew not whether to laugh or cry when I

114

read it, and considered all the excellent work he has done in the past. Allow me to give you a little more brandy, Dr Onslow.'

Onslow did not like to accept a gift at the hands of an atheist, but he needed another drink, and so he handed over his glass and thanked him. When Anstey-Ward came back, Onslow said:

'I have not read the book to which you refer, but I have heard it described.

'Have you?'

'I can only say that it did not sound half so ridiculous as *Vestiges of Creation*.'

This very popular book had argued in favour of an immeasurably ancient earth and the transmutation of species. Louisa, influenced by Primrose, had been greatly taken with it just before she married Onslow, who had gently persuaded her that it was nonsense. To Onslow now, the mention of *Vestiges* brought back sharp memories of the days of his courtship, the early days of his head-mastership. He looked at Anstey-Ward and went on:

'You, I suppose, have respect for that work? You believe that clover springs up spontaneously where lime is spread? Oh, and that oats can grow where rye has been spread, or was it the other way about?'

Anstey-Ward's eyebrows drew together over his nose.

'No, I don't, and neither do I believe in dogs playing dominoes. Your sarcasm is misplaced, sir. I thought that book as foolish as you did, and so did every man with the least scientific knowledge.'

'Nonetheless I was informed by an acquaintance of mine, a clergyman but a scientist, sir, that it was written not by Lord Byron's daughter or the Prince Consort but by a Mr Darwin, an eminent naturalist so I am told.'

'Mr Darwin is indeed an eminent naturalist, and he is not the author of any such piece of trash,' said Anstey-Ward. He had heard from a fellow member of the British Association that Mr Darwin was at work on a serious theory of transmutation, but he did not consider Onslow the scoffer to be worthy of being told this.

115

'I am not a man of science,' said Onslow, 'and I know only that the greater number of scientists are persuaded that their investigations present no lasting threat to revealed truth. Why, the greater number of them believe that our world had a catastrophic origin – the idea that it had not is merely a passing scientific fad, like, like the theory of phlogiston. For my part I am persuaded that the day will come when the earth is proved to be little older than was thought by Archbishop Ussher.'

By this he meant two or three million years – infinitely more than the Church had once insisted and infinitely less than most geologists supposed. Looking at Anstey-Ward's face, which seemed to him smugly contemptuous, he went on:

'It is my belief that one day all the incompatibilities between doctrine and the seeming results of scientific investigations will be smoothed out. Even the difference between what we are now said to know of the earth's origin, and what we are told in Genesis, will be as nothing once we know more. A little learning is a dangerous thing, Dr Anstey-Ward, and it is a little, a very little learning that our geologists and naturalists possess.' He finished: 'I shall wait until it is at last discovered that revelation was never wrong.'

'You'll wait a long time, Dr Onslow. Are you indeed telling me that you hold by every belief I had thought all intelligent Christians jettisoned more than twenty years ago – the universal flood, the creation of 4004 BC? Surely not!'

'Not precisely,' said Onslow, 'I will own that I do not believe the flood was universal, but as to the age of the earth, yes, I cannot believe it is anything like so old as you geologists maintain. It is inconceivable that our Lord created the world hundreds of millions of years before he created man, for whose sake it was made. In short, while I reject Archbishop Ussher's calculation in detail, I accept its spirit.' Onslow was expressing himself so firmly because in Anstey-Ward's company, his need to hold on to the old Christian certainties was intense. He almost wished he had said that he did simply accept that the world had been

116

created in 4004 BC. It seemed almost like toadying to meet Anstey-Ward half way, and he would rather anything, in the circumstances, than be thought a toady.

'You shock me,' said Anstey-Ward, very gravely. 'I had not thought it possible.' He believed that Onslow was probably modifying his real views because he did not want a quarrel, and thus he thought that Onslow was as much an intellectual monster as a sensual monster: doubly unfit to be either a headmaster or a bishop.

'Yes, for you see, I am not one to reject the traditional teaching of the church lightly, no matter what havoc the hammers of the geologists may wreak. I will not replace the wisdom of two thousand years with the wisdom, if one can call it that, of less than a hundred.' In asserting this, Onslow was asserting his moral worth, which existed in spite of everything.

'And do you reverence the Bible as you reverence the traditions of the Church?' said Anstey-Ward. 'I'm aware that not all clergymen do so.'

'Most certainly I do.'

'Then I'll quote the Bible to you – "all the rivers run into the sea, yet the sea is not full. Unto the place from whence the rivers come, thither they return again. The thing that hath been, it is that which shall be; and that which is done, is that which shall be done, and there is no new thing under the sun". As neat a statement of the uniformitarian and gradualist position as you could find.'

Onslow was horrified to hear an infidel quote his favourite Ecclesiastes, which in secret he loved because it was not specifically Christian. He could only think to say:

'You forget that other parts of the Bible are equally true.'

Anstey-Ward's moment of frivolity was past. He said:

'Well Dr Onslow, all I can say is that so far from living to see reconciliation between Genesis and geology, you will very likely live to see all manner of scientific revelations which to your mind will be blasphemous. Science and religion are growing further apart day by day. I know the kind of scientists you mean, who pooh-pooh any little difficulty, but they are wrong.'

117

'Are they indeed?'

Anstey-Ward got up and fetched himself a third brandy, forgetting to offer one to Onslow. 'I tell you sir,' he said while he was pouring it out, and Onslow could not see him, 'the day is not far off when you will be forced to acknowledge not only what men less – sure of themselves have acknowledged for years, but that your first ancestor was very likely an orang-outan.'

It was dislike of Onslow which made Anstey-Ward take up this extreme position. In reality, he believed Lamarck's speculation about the origin of the human race to be a somewhat wild one, and was rarely prepared to say unequivocally that he believed in the transmutation of species. Theories of transmutation and theories of immutability seemed to him equally difficult, and though he inclined towards the transmutationists, he had his doubts. For one thing, it seemed unlikely that the three great races of mankind could have descended from a common ancestor in the comparatively short time since humanity appeared on earth, as Onslow would have maintained they had: they must have arisen separately, for the cunning and idiocy of the Mongolian and Negroid races placed them so very far below the White.

'I never,' said Onslow gently, 'in all my life heard any suggestion so absurd. The immeasurable gulf between ourselves and the beasts is alone proof of a divine and special creation of man, and so, I know, would any scientist not blinded by infidelity agree.' The suggestion that he might be descended from an ape would have sickened him had he not thought it altogether ludicrous.

'Not *any* scientist,' said Anstey-Ward, feeling himself to be on insecure ground. 'There are certainly many who reject the idea of transmutation, but if ever they accept it they will none of them dream of exempting man from its workings.' He doubted this, but was not going to admit to Onslow that scientists could balk at facts they considered unpleasant. 'Are your own certainties not in the least disturbed by the great resemblance there is between apes and men? especially between apes and black men?'

118

'Great resemblance! What resemblance? Do you call a hideous parody of the physical man a resemblance? It is the mind, the spirit, the soul that signifies, and even black men have a soul.'

'I don't think it is that which signifies at all,' said Anstey-Ward. 'Do you know, the older I grow, the less respect I have for the mind and spirit and soul of man. The animals manage their lives with a good deal less trouble. Has it never occurred to you that beasts never sin?'

'Naturally it has occurred to me – you forget I am a Christian, Dr Anstey-Ward. The capacity to sin is proof of our superiority, proof that God gave us free will and the knowledge of good and evil, as he did not to the beasts.'

Suddenly they both remembered Onslow's capacity to sin.

'Allow me to give you a little more brandy,' said Anstey-Ward. 'I see your glass is empty.'

'Thank you.' Onslow closed his eyes and bit his lip when Anstey-Ward could no longer see him. He was sure that his opponent would produce the 'documents' as soon as he had given him his brandy, and he waited wretchedly.

Anstey-Ward did consider at last bringing up the matter which Onslow had come down to Wiltshire to discuss, but he shrank from the thought, for he felt both too tired and too close to being drunk to be as dignified as the occasion required. An idea came to him, and he seized it. Instead of mentioning the letters, he said in a voice which was almost cheerful:

'Would you object to telling me what you thought of Mr Mansel's *Bampton Lectures*, Dr Onslow? I think we can discuss those rather more profitably than we can transmutation, and the age of the earth.'

It was so unexpected that Onslow nearly laughed.

'I can't conceive why you should wish to know, sir, and I am surprised that a man of your opinions should have taken any interest in them, but I can only tell you that I thought them the most impressive piece of theological argument since Paley – words for our time.'

These sermon-lectures, recently published, had been the

intellectual sensation of the previous year. Mr Mansel was a philosopher and clergyman who had used eloquence and logic to show that it was not so much impious as nonsensical, essentially irrational, to attempt to make limited human reason comprehend the Infinite. It was therefore irrational to doubt the morality of God's ordering Abraham to kill his son, on the grounds that such an action appeared wicked to the human mind. The goodness of God must necessarily be too high and remote for human understanding; mere rational understanding, he confessed at one point, made the atheist position the most plausible. But it was not so, and the wise who used their reason well would inevitably end in bowing down before the revelations provided by God, no matter how difficult they seemed.

Anstey-Ward had been pleased, and some simple Christians worried, by the remarks about atheism, but many of the intellectual orthodox considered that Mansel had coldly and brilliantly vanquished such nervous Broad Churchmen as Martin Primrose and Frederick Denison Maurice.

'I thought you might,' said Anstey-Ward. 'For my part I agree with whoever it was said he is like the man sitting on an inn-sign, sawing busily. So you think, sir, that there is a morality high above what we consider to be moral – which allows what we consider to be wicked to be in fact good?'

After a moment, Onslow saw where the conversation was tending, understood why Anstey-Ward had raised this unexpected topic. Yet he was astonished by an atheist's seeming to be concerned by what was moral. Straightening his shoulders and controlling his voice, he defended himself against the hint that he thought fit to ignore common morality, and fancied himself to be obeying a higher law when he sinned. He said:

'I will not dispute with you about the nature and the actions of a God in Whom you do not believe, sir. He has made us know how it is we are to act through His Son and His New Testament. What He demands of man is what man must deliver.'

'I see,' said Anstey-Ward. 'Yet you must be bound to consider God's actions better than man's, for all that, must

120

you not? And I don't know that a man who thinks the hewing of Agag in pieces to be far from a crime can be said to possess anything but a twisted morality.'

'Forgive me for saying that you are blinded by your prejudices,' said Onslow.

'I forgive you that,' said Anstey-Ward, and looked at him.

19

Louisa lay awake in bed, waiting for her husband and thinking of how passionately she wanted him to become a bishop: not merely any bishop, but Bishop of Ipswich. She had almost rather that than see him Archbishop of Canterbury, for Ipswich was her father's old see, and she had spent a happy childhood in the palace there. This childhood home she wanted to recreate largely because she still missed her father, though it was eleven years since his death. It was a continuing grief to her that she could not visit his grave, which was in Palestine – he had died of cholera on a trip to the Holy Land in 1848, a year after her own marriage, and had been succeeded at Ipswich by an old man who might at any moment die and give Onslow his opportunity, were it not for Anstey-Ward.

To help keep her mind off the immediate issue, about which she could do nothing till Onslow came upstairs, Louisa began to think about her marriage, and to compare her husband with her father, something she had not done directly before.

Louisa remembered how when she was a small child her father used to throw her up in the air and catch her, making her laugh at being safe again after an adventure. And when she grew to adulthood, she saw in George Onslow a man who would be able to take care of her as her father had: an older husband, best friend of her best-loved brother, destined for a high place in the church. He was kind and indulgent except when he was in a very bad humour, and just like her father, he tried to shelter her from all that was unpleasant, to which she had no objection. But she could

122

not imagine her father being angry when she turned out not to have been successfully sheltered, as Onslow had been when she revealed that she knew. Yet perhaps, she thought, her father too would have been rather shocked to learn that she was able to look on unpleasantness with cool and open eyes when she could not avoid it.

At the time of her marriage, Louisa had not seen in Onslow a younger substitute for her ageing father, for the two men did not look at all alike. She had simply thought Onslow as dashing as it was possible for a thirty-year-old clergyman to be, and had greatly enjoyed the sensation of being sufficiently grown-up to be married. Yet in spite of the excitement she had felt at eighteen, it had taken her many years to think of herself as truly grown-up. Considering the matter now, she wondered whether she had not thought of herself almost as a child masquerading in adult clothes until the day before yesterday, when her time of trial came, and to her own surprise she had almost welcomed it.

In spite of Onslow's odd tastes and occasional bad temper, she had felt safe with him till that moment when she saw him read Anstey-Ward's letter and guessed what it was. And she was even now unable to believe that Anstey-Ward would carry out his threat to deprive Onslow of all high preferment. Such things, she thought, did not happen.

Suddenly she thought of how she wanted a baby, and had been denied one: it was the only true dissatisfaction of her life till now. She would certainly feel entirely adult if she became a mother, and Onslow would acknowledge her as such – but it was perhaps odd that performing certain duties of a wife had not had that effect. She and Onslow embraced, as she called it to herself, perhaps once in three weeks, and she had no idea whether that was much more or much less than other couples. In spite of all her present anxiety, sensuous feelings began to creep round Louisa's loins as she thought of embraces, and she blushed, for she and Onslow never spoke of these things. They pretended that nothing happened between them that might not happen between brother and sister, and that, she thought, was perhaps why what they sometimes did together had no effect on their lives outside the bedroom, and did not make her feel like a full-blown woman.

At that moment, Onslow opened the door, and Louisa jumped.

'I thought to find you asleep,' he said, looking at her as he set his candle down. His tone of voice was forbidding, but Louisa took no notice.

'What happened? What did he say?'

There was a pause, then Onslow said:

'We spent out time discussing Mr Mansel's *Bampton Lectures*.'

'What?'

'We made a tacit agreement to leave other matters till the morning. Please, Louisa, do not question me. You will know all in due course, and I am very tired.'

Onslow removed his coat, took his nightshirt, and retired behind a screen to undress. Louisa, bewildered, said at last:

'But please, Dr Onslow, tell me a little. That is – were you in agreement about the *Bampton Lectures*? Was it a friendly discussion?'

Louisa did not share her husband's view of Mr Mansel. Like her brother, she thought that to say God might act in a way contrary to ordinary ideas of morality was to deprive the concept of goodness of all meaning. She therefore simply refused to believe that God had ordered Joshua to massacre the Canaanites, or Abraham to kill his son.

'No, we were not in agreement, nor was it a very friendly discussion.'

'Oh, dear. What did you say? Does Dr Anstey-Ward agree with Martin?' She did not like to say 'and me'.

'Louisa my dear, please go to sleep. I cannot discuss it any further.'

'How can I possibly simply go to sleep? George, I insist on your telling me.'

'And I insist on holding my tongue for the meanwhile.'

After a moment, Louisa said:

'Very well.' Lying down slowly in the bed, she decided it

would not be wise to press him further, for it seemed matters were at a very delicate stage. If they had spent their time discussing indifferent and intellectual matters, she thought, there must be hope, even though they had disagreed. It was likely that all would be well without her having to lift a finger: she felt a little twinge of disappointment.

As soon as his wife submitted, Onslow felt a great longing to tell her every detail of his unfortunate conversation with Anstey-Ward. He passionately desired Louisa's sympathy, but he forced himself to be silent for the time being, because he must preserve his energies for what was to come tomorrow.

═══

Next morning, Anstey-Ward woke very early, after a night of surprisingly untroubled sleep. He rose and dressed himself, and then went out into the grey cold garden, hoping to prepare himself mentally for the coming encounter – but as he wandered slowly round, he thought not so much of what was to happen between himself and Onslow as of Christian and why he had sent him to Charton, and so brought all this down upon his head.

It was worldliness, he supposed, the simple snobbish desire for his son to have the education of a gentleman. But he wondered whether he would have obeyed the dictates of snobbery had Christian shown any interest in science; and tugging at his whiskers, he pictured the son he would have had in the event of his being kept away from public school.

Had he stayed at home, Christian would have had no clerical tutor to introduce him to Homer and Horace and the other bores. He would have had a scientific and useful education, as Rose had had, and as a result would have been curious and practical instead of dreamy. He might not even have learnt classics enough to take him to Oxford, thought Anstey-Ward in a sudden new loathing of the established system of education. He remembered Christian's remarks about the quite incredible ignorance of Charton boys thought good scholars: ignorance of the whereabouts of Moscow, and of who wrote *King Lear*, to say nothing of their ignorance of the earth's history. Anstey-Ward thought he would not be surprised to learn that Dr Onslow thought Moscow was in Persia, and taught his boys the same with a neat sneering half-smile on his face.

The entire system, thought Anstey-Ward, was corrupt; and as he thought this, he paused by a yew hedge and saw strung across it a dew-laden net of spider's web, in which there was a gnat entangled. His thoughts took a different direction. He supposed that some might compare Onslow with the gnat, yet he felt rather that he himself could be so compared, that it was he who had flown into a sticky and elastic net of a world where people of importance would tolerate any fault committed by one of their number so long as there was no scandal. Onslow's sins, he thought suddenly, would be considered very venial by most of those classically educated men who sat in the Cabinet, or even on the bench of bishops. They would not hound Onslow out of the country simply because they knew, not if their knowledge were private.

Anstey-Ward had once thought of himself as the representative of acknowledged decency, with cohorts of good opinion ranged behind him, but now, when he was about to confront Onslow, he could not think of himself like that. He felt, if not entangled and at hopeless odds with the world, at least very much alone. For he would not have the power to make scandal unless certain of the great chose to let him, and he imagined that in the case of so enormous a potential scandal the editors of influential newspapers might not so choose. The thought of this was enough to make him long to create such a scandal, make him hope that Onslow would issue a challenge by refusing his terms. Yet at the same time that was what he most dreaded, a contemptuous 'Publish and be damned' – for if he succeeded in exposing Onslow, he would also be exposing Christian's part in the affair. It was that consideration which had held him back at the start from deciding to ruin Onslow publicly.

He turned away from the yew hedge, and walked back towards the house. Approaching it, he looked up towards the window of the bedroom where Onslow and his wife had passed the night – and there he saw Onslow, in his nightshirt, looking down at him. Their eyes remained fixed on each other for some seconds, then Onslow quickly turned away. Anstey-Ward guessed that he would dress himself and come down immediately: the confrontation would take place before breakfast. He went into his library to wait.

Onslow dressed and shaved himself in haste, thankful that Louisa was still asleep. It was best, he thought, to discuss the matter before everyone else was up – he wondered whether Anstey-Ward had passed as disturbed a night as he had, unable to stop examining the evening's conversation and thinking of all the things he might have said. Now he planned what he was going to say upon entering the library. His stomach churned painfully at the thought that he was at last about to set eyes on the 'documents', and he found his old hope growing inside him, the hope that they would turn out not to be irrefutable evidence, not to be words in his own hand.

As soon as he was dressed he went downstairs. He found the library door wide open, and Anstey-Ward sitting in full view. Entering, and closing the door behind him, he spoke the words he had rehearsed to himself before the other had a chance to say anything.

'Dr Anstey-Ward, I wish to see the documents to which you referred in your letter. I think you will not deny it is my right to do so.'

Anstey-Ward lowered Gosse's *History of the British Sea-Anemones and Corals*, which he picked out of the bookcase at random, and of which he had not read a word.

'No, I won't deny it. Pray sit down, sir.'

Onslow took a chair. Anstey-Ward went over to his desk and took out his watch-chain, to which there was a bunch of keys attached. He unlocked one of the drawers. Out of it Onslow saw him take a piece of paper which even at a distance looked as though it had spent months in a trouser-pocket, a neat piece of cheap-looking paper, and a folded square of cream-laid. He came over, and handed them to him in silence.

127

Onslow opened out the first piece of paper, the very shabby one, which was the note Arthur Bright had written to Christian in chapel. As he read it, and gradually took in its meaning, his hands shook: it had never crossed his mind that Arthur might deliberately have told another boy, and told him in such a fashion, only to enliven a sermon he thought dull. Yet while he was coping with this new knowledge, another part of his mind was busily thinking that this was a mere allegation, not proof − but then he came to Bright's mention of an extract from one of his own letters. He forced himself to open the folded square of good paper.

There were the words in his own hand, referring to his darling's beauty and the sofa, and it was worse than he had imagined.

'Would you like a glass of water, Dr Onslow?' said Anstey-Ward, honestly concerned, for Onslow looked white enough to faint like a woman.

'No,' said Onslow, slowly re-folding the pieces of paper, and slipping them into his inside pocket.

'I am sorry,' said Anstey-Ward. He thought it was ridiculous for him to be saying so, yet he meant it, for he felt much as Onslow did when called upon to flog a boy who could not be stoical.

There was silence for some time. Then Onslow said:

'Your terms remain the same?' He could think of nothing better to say, not now that he knew what Bright had done.

'They do, sir.'

'I accept them.'

They had both imagined vaguely that they would have a long conversation, its length proportionate to its importance, yet now it was over.

Onslow got up to go. His legs felt only just strong enough to bear him. As he reached the door, Anstey-Ward said:

'Oh, Dr Onslow, you still have those letters in your pocket.'

'Yes?'

'Pray give them back to me.'

Their eyes met. Then Onslow took them out and laid them on the table.

20

'I am afraid it will be just such another miserable day as yesterday,' said Chatty, pouring out tea.

'Yes, I am afraid you are right,' said Louisa, who because she had not seen him till they sat down to breakfast, guessed that Onslow had already had his interview with Anstey-Ward. She supposed that her husband had spent a long time in conversation with him – she did not know that unable to face her, he had spent half an hour on the chilly verandah, having nowhere else to go but the bedroom he shared with her.

'Miss Anstey-Ward,' said Onslow, who had worried his wife by saying almost nothing till now, 'Mrs Onslow and I must leave you very soon after breakfast. Would it be possible for us to hire a conveyance to take us to the station from somewhere round about?'

'Oh! But hiring a conveyance is not at all necessary. We have just set up our own carriage, which can very easily take you – it is such a convenience to have one's own carriage.' Chatty had been pressing her brother to set one up for years.

'I should hate to be without one, I own,' said Louisa, and refrained from glancing at Anstey-Ward, who had the power to deprive her of the means of keeping a carriage.

'We are much obliged to you, Miss Anstey-Ward,' said Onslow. He was thinking of how he would tell Louisa everything as soon as they were on their way, now that he had to some extent mastered his sense of shame.

Anstey-Ward, like Onslow, thought that all these civilities were even more painful than those uttered yesterday.

129

Yet now all was over, he hated Onslow less than he had done, and so he wondered why this should be so. With an effort he said:

'We shall be very glad indeed to convey you to the station, Dr Onslow,' and all his listeners were faintly embarrassed by a polite remark made too late.

The meal finally came to an end. Chatty stayed in the breakfast-parlour, Anstey-Ward went once more to the library, and the Onslows, making excuses, went upstairs. Once they were in their room, Onslow said:

'I have spoken to him.' Having avoided Louisa before breakfast, he now felt he could not wait even till they were on their way to Salisbury. He also suspected that she guessed what had happened, and would in any case demand to be told. He could not put her off a second time.

'Oh Dr Onslow, tell me.'

'He is implacable. There is nothing else to say.'

'Oh no,' said Louisa, putting a hand to her cheek. 'No, I can't believe it.'

'It is what we expected, after all. Is it not?'

'No.' She meant it: she had been entirely convinced that a compromise would be settled on, such as a not too immediate resignation followed by the acceptance of a bishopric, or at least a deanery. At last she said, not looking at Onslow: 'The documents he spoke of – what were they?'

He blushed at the mention of them.

'Evidence I could not dispute.' Then there was a pause, and Onslow took out his watch and examined it. He said at length: 'It is less than it might be. I must be thankful there is to be no scandal.' He thought what excellent control he was keeping, and pictured himself abandoning it.

'I suppose so,' muttered Louisa, in whose mind a plan was quickly forming.

Raising her head, ignoring the hand he stretched out to her, she told him that he must excuse her and then went out of the room. Onslow supposed she was going to answer a call of nature, and was angry with her for having one at such a moment.

Louisa sped downstairs and went straight to the library,

130

into which she had seen Anstey-Ward disappear. She knocked on the door and heard his surprised-sounding voice calling 'Come in.'

'Why, Mrs Onslow!' he said when she entered, though the knock had given him an idea of who it was. Chatty would not have knocked, and he could not think that Onslow would have done so. 'What can I do for you, ma'am? Pray sit down!' he said, as he had said to her husband earlier. He got up and placed a chair for her, which she accepted. Then she said:

'You can do a great deal for me, Dr Anstey-Ward. I have come to ask you to be a little less harsh towards my husband.'

He started. She folded her hands neatly in her lap, and there was silence.

'Dr Onslow does not know I have come down to talk to you,' Louisa offered as Anstey-Ward said nothing. 'I am hoping you will listen to a wife's plea.' She knew her words were melodramatic, but her tone was light. Anstey-Ward, shocked though he was, rather liked the touch of melodrama. It was something outside the whole range of his experience.

'I don't know what you mean by a little less harsh, ma'am,' he said, wishing he could think of something better to say. He wondered just how much she knew, whether Onslow had fobbed her off with some story.

'Will you not let him remain at Charton till Christmas?' she said, leaning forward. Louisa was keeping her voice under strict control, just as Onslow had kept his. 'Then, you see, if he informs the trustees of his coming resignation now, it will not look in any way odd. I am sure you are as desirous of preventing disagreeable gossip as we are, Dr Anstey-Ward.'

Anstey-Ward looked at her face and realised that Louisa knew everything, that she was no such sheltered innocent as he, far more than Onslow, thought all women should be. All her light conversation of last night, and at breakfast, had been a mere act – he felt a fool for having supposed there was a need to deceive her as much as Chatty.

Distressed though he was by her duplicity, Anstey-Ward was also relieved: for to have her understand like a man was better than to have her ask him awkward questions, as had been his fear when she first came into the room. And he would not feel like a merciless brute, denying the requests of a woman who knew. Yet on the other hand, he thought, it was dreadful not to do whatever he could to comfort a guiltless creature who for all her boldness, must have suffered terribly when her husband confessed.

In his conflict, Anstey-Ward said nothing, but only watched her, waiting to learn more.

'I do not think I could bear it if there were such gossip,' she said. 'You will understand that, I am very sure, Dr Anstey-Ward.'

He decided there was nothing for it but to talk to her as though this were a perfectly ordinary situation. He said:

'Yes indeed, but Mrs Onslow, I do not see that Dr Onslow's leaving Charton at the end of this half-year need give rise to gossip of the kind you mean. He has only to plead ill-health.'

Louisa thought this excuse would be extremely likely to lead to gossip, for Onslow was so healthy that he had not contracted an infectious complaint, not even influenza, since he was a child. His stomach was absolutely sound, and occasional migraines were the only illness to which he was subject.

'I am afraid everyone would know that was untrue, sir.'

'No, no,' he assured her. 'There are any number of diseases from which men who appear perfectly healthy may suffer. I suggest severe and persistent migraine.' It was unfortunate that he picked on this condition. 'That would account also for his refusal to accept high preferment – he would be thinking the work would be too much for him.' He added, clearing his throat: 'I take it you know what I have required of Dr Onslow.'

'I know,' said Louisa. 'Yes, I do know. But as for ill-health being a sufficient excuse for his refusing high preferment, it might serve with regard to a bishopric, but a dean has no work to speak of. A deanery would be the very

132

thing for him in those circumstances. Dr Anstey-Ward, will you not compromise even so far as to allow him to accept a deanery? Only to prevent disagreeable talk? You insist on his resigning immediately, will you not even grant me this?'

'I'm sorry, but I cannot go back on what I have said, Mrs Onslow.'

'Then you are condemning us both to a life of wretchedness,' she said, quite gently.

'Forgive me, but I've yet to learn that the life of a parish clergyman is one of wretchedness.'

Changing tack, Louisa said, still softly and reasonably:

'What have *I* done to deserve this? Is it right that I should be punished too? You see I am quite frank with you.'

Anstey-Ward did not like to point out that she had accepted Onslow for better for worse, and so he simply looked at her, and fiddled with his watch-chain. In spite of his stern view of the marriage vow, he did feel it was dreadful to ruin Louisa as well as her husband – it was only that he saw no alternative.

'I'm sorry, Mrs Onslow,' he said at last. 'But I ought to tell you that it is largely for your sake I do not wish to make a scandal out of this. Were it not for you I might think otherwise.'

'I suppose I must thank you for that. I do thank you.'

There was a pause. Then Louisa said:

'You know, Dr Anstey-Ward, my husband has sincerely repented of his error.'

'I'm glad to hear that, Mrs Onslow.'

'In the circumstances, is it right for you to insist on having your way? He is in such agony of mind.' She added: 'I daresay he did not tell you so, but then he is very proud. He would never tell you that he had repented.'

'I know, ma'am.'

'Dr Anstey-Ward, precisely what right have you to condemn him in this way? I ask you that in all seriousness, not to be insulting. Do you indeed have the right to judge him? Like God?'

Anstey-Ward took out his watch and wound it.

'I'm not sure, Mrs Onslow. But however that may be, I –'

'You acknowledge that you have not. Oh, Dr Anstey-Ward, you know it is not Christian to behave in this way.'

'I don't know about that,' he said. 'Christians have behaved in all manner of ways.'

Louisa leant forward in her chair, and made a concession. 'Perhaps, perhaps you do have the right to ask him to resign from Charton, where he is open to temptation, but do you have the right as a fellow Christian to punish him in other ways? Can you not leave vengeance to God? When Dr Onslow is so bitterly repentant, so determined never to err again? Oh, Dr Anstey-Ward, please listen to me!'

He was now looking at her eager, anxious, pretty face, and the expression on his own face was miserable. She could see that her persistence was softening him at last.

'You know in your heart that you do not have the right to cause so much unhappiness,' she said.

'Perhaps not,' he said, 'yet I still cannot think it right for Dr Onslow to hold a high position in the church. And I don't think it right that a clergyman should be quite so ambitious.'

Louisa ignored this last remark, and said:

'But think of the great good he has done since he came to Charton. In many ways he is the best of headmasters. Is he not as much entitled to a reward for the good he has done as he is entitled to be punished for his fault?'

Anstey-Ward said nothing: he knew that Onslow had done much good.

'Dr Anstey-Ward, I suspect you of being a kind man at heart. Can I not appeal to your kindness as well as to your sense of what is right?'

Anstey-Ward got up from his chair and walked rapidly towards the window, for it was terrible to hear Louisa voice his conscientious doubts – and he did like to think of himself as a kindly, tolerant and generous man. Seeing him rise, Louisa rose too, sure that she was on the point of victory, or at least of achieving a compromise. She said, quite lightly:

'Is it right for you to punish him so severely for such a little weakness, so small a fault?'

Then he turned round and faced her again.

'It is not so small a fault, Mrs Onslow. You are mistaken.'

She could see that she had said the wrong thing: Anstey-Ward's tone of voice was very firm.

'But you will own. . .' she began.

'Mrs Onslow, your husband's fault is a very grave one, and whether I have the right or not, what I am doing is just. I do not wish to hurt you, that's the last thing I want, but it is a question of justice.'

She could not bear the thought that triumph had eluded her so narrowly, and as Anstey-Ward went back towards his chair, she threw herself down on her knees in one last desperate move. It was as though she had never before truly wanted Onslow to be a bishop.

'Dr Anstey-Ward, I promise you on my honour as a Christian woman that Dr Onslow's peculiarities have never interfered with his running of the school. Can you not have a little pity?'

'Mrs Onslow, I beg you! Pray get up now!'

'He has been the best of headmasters, the boys love him, is it indeed right to wreck the rest of his life?'

'Please, please! This is useless, ma'am, I cannot think your husband fit to be a schoolmaster, nor a clergyman either!'

At that moment, Onslow opened the library door, and stepped in, and saw his wife kneeling there. On her tear-streaked face there was an expression of guilty surprise. For a moment they all looked at one another in silence, then Onslow took two paces forward and said icily:

'Get up, Mrs Onslow.'

Anstey-Ward thought Onslow was being harsh: in spite of his intransigence, he was moved by the sight of this delicate bishop's daughter on her knees.

'Get up.'

Louisa attempted to obey him, but her skirts and the

stays that made her breathless made it difficult for her to rise without help when she was exhausted by emotion.

'Help me,' she muttered.

Anstey-Ward took a step forward, but retreated at a look from Onslow, who assisted his wife with the air of one touching dirt. When Louisa was on her feet again, Anstey-Ward said awkwardly:

'I would like to say a few words to Mrs Onslow. They may be painful for you to hear, Dr Onslow.'

Onslow said: 'Are you asking me to go out of the room and leave you to continue the tête-à-tête you are enjoying?'

'You might say that.'

Onslow turned away from him, not condescending to make any reply, and Anstey-Ward coloured angrily. He wanted very much to explain to Louisa why her husband's was not so small a fault, explain that she had been misled and that he was not so unjustly vengeful as she supposed.

'I shall be glad,' said Onslow, 'if you will be good enough to have your carriage brought round. It is time we were gone.'

Anstey-Ward pulled the bell in silence in response to this arrogant request, and as he did so, he assured himself that he had found the perfect solution, whatever Louisa might think.

21

Once it was certain beyond all doubt that they were to be driven into obscurity, the Onslows felt bound together as they never had before. They did not speak on the drive into Salisbury, or on the station platform, but as soon as the train pulled out and they were on their way to London, Onslow said:

'I hope you are satisfied.'

'In what way satisfied?' said Louisa, taking out a book with unsteady hands. She had guessed that Onslow would attack her, though there was no precedent for such an attack.

'By grovelling in that way you have disgraced me utterly. Do you realise that?'

'I do not think so.'

'Do you not realise that he believes I stooped so low as to send you to beg on my behalf?'

'I told him you had not.' I will not cry, thought Louisa.

'He now holds me in indescribable contempt, and I cannot blame him.'

'I am sure he does not,' Louisa replied, her voice quavering a little. Full of a sense of her own humiliation, she thought Onslow ought to be comforting her, thanking her for her brave, foolish, failed attempt to do what she could for him. 'At least, not more so than before.'

He gasped, then said:

'How dared you mention my business with him at all? How dared you betray you knew anything about it? I

137

took you with me so that you might – it was no affair of yours.'

'But it was an affair of mine,' said Louisa, speaking more firmly than before. She stopped pretending to read. 'It was very much my affair!'

'You are mistaken, Mrs Onslow.'

His addressing her as that made her throw her book on the floor in a sudden rage which astonished her.

'I am to be ruined with you, and you say it is no business of mine. How dare you?'

He was taken aback by her furious tone, but he did not betray it.

'Your business is most certainly not to interfere.'

'You seem to forget, Dr Onslow,' she said deliberately, and she would have risen up and stood over him had it not been for the jerking of the train, 'that it is your misdeeds which have brought us to this pass. Not mine. And you try to maintain that it is my effort to save us at the last which has led to our disgrace, not your behaviour. Well, I will not tolerate it.'

'Oh! So now at last you reproach me! Now you show what you think of me!'

'Yes, I reproach you! Do you understand that because of your inability to control your passions my life is to be spoilt for ever? Do you ever think of that?' Her bosom rose and fell as though propelled by steam, and her face was scarlet. She had quite forgotten that Onslow had expressed keen and bitter regret for this on the day she told him that she knew.

Onslow was as white as she was flushed, but his anger was no longer cold, it was as hot as hers.

'What a great mistake I made in marrying you,' he said. 'You are a woman without even self-control.'

'Yes! And I in marrying you! I cannot begin to express my dislike of you.'

'I might well say the same.'

Neither of them felt any sense of release after expressing their feelings: having said the worst they could, they felt poisoned. All they could do was settle down for the rest of

138

the journey, and wonder whether they could ever be reconciled after this, their first true quarrel.

———

During the next few days, Onslow could not bring himself to tell Louisa quite how bad their situation was, for fear of what she might say and he might say back to her. For his part, painful though it was to think of their financial position, he preferred it to dwelling on other matters, such as Bright, and sin, and God.

He supposed his wife did not know that ever since he became headmaster, he had speculated on the stock exchange, always hoping to make a fortune which would support him when he retired, a fortune which he would need if he did not draw some great plum such as the bishopric of Durham or Winchester. He had had a few successes, but far more reverses, for though he enjoyed the game of speculation, he had no talent for it. His predecessor as Headmaster of Charton was rumoured to have saved nearly forty thousand pounds, but out of his six thousand a year Onslow had saved less than nine all told, and he could only be thankful that he was not in debt. He remembered how he had nearly decided to resign last year, when Bright left, and when Anstey-Ward knew nothing, but had not done so because of the money: it had been his intention to remain another three or four years at Charton and during that period to invest as much as he could in Government funds. He had succeeded in saving some two thousand pounds, but had not carried out his intention to the full, for the temptation to speculate and make a fortune quickly was very great. And he had been sure that he would spend very little time, if any, as a dean with a thousand a year. He had been sure that he would soon be a bishop with five.

Louisa, thought Onslow, would have to curb her extravagance once they were limited to the eight or nine hundred a year which a good living might produce. One day she would have to be told so, but he could not bear to think of it. It was hard enough to face the reality himself.

139

He did not think that Louisa had already realised the necessity for saving money, nor did he stop to consider that she never had been truly extravagant, that she had never asked him for a penny more than he was willing to give her. In his mind she was, at least by the standards of the Primrose family, a very frivolous creature, and he had not censured her for being so till now. He had once liked to indulge her, and had not only made her a generous allowance but had bought expensive presents for her. He liked women to be elegant, and if only by refraining from comment, he had encouraged her to dress more fashionably than sober people thought proper for a clergyman's wife. It now seemed to him, after his quarrel with her, that it was impossible he could ever have taken pleasure in having a well-dressed wife.

They did not talk to each other except when it was strictly necessary. Louisa never asked after his letter of resignation to the trustees (which pleaded ill-health because that was the obvious excuse) and he never asked her how she was explaining to those who came to call on her that they were leaving (she preferred to say that her impulsive husband thought fifteen years as Headmaster was long enough). Above all, neither talked about Primrose, though he was constantly in both their minds, and what to tell him would have been the first thing they discussed had it not been for their quarrel.

Onslow wrote to Primrose, telling him the whole truth including about the quarrel, before he even wrote to the trustees. It was the most difficult letter he had ever had to write. It was long, and very calm but for the last paragraph, in which Onslow acknowledged that Primrose must feel wholly deceived in his friend, and might well be unable to forgive him. Yet he begged his forgiveness, and begged him also to come to Charton as soon as he could.

On July 23rd, he had a reply. Primrose forgave him, Primrose was coming. Onslow made himself go straight to tell his wife, who burst into tears; and alone in his study, he wept too.

22

'I have had Dr Anstey-Ward's reply to my letter,' said Primrose, entering Onslow's study. He had been at Charton a week, and had agreed to correspond with Anstey-Ward on Onslow's behalf: Onslow felt unable to do this himself, but the humiliating task had to be accomplished. 'The gist of it is that in view of your financial difficulties, he has no objection to your accepting a preferment of up to twelve hundred a year, so long as it is not a deanery.' Primrose did not add that Anstey-Ward had emphasised that this was for Louisa's sake, for he had thought that insistence canting.

'How very generous, in a world where as soon as a lesser preferment which happens to be generously endowed falls in, the Ecclesiastical Commissioners cut it down at once.'

'Don't be bitter, George. There are still many rectories worth oh, over a thousand, even after being cut down. And a canonry may be the same, though of course they are less easily to be had than formerly. If you could combine a living with a prebendal stall – .'

'Yes, you are right, I am too bitter, and peevish.'

'If it is the thought of Louisa that disturbs you, I have spoken to her, and she perfectly understands that she must make stringent economies, comparatively speaking.' He added: 'The fact is, she appears to have known more of your misfortunes on the stock exchange than you guessed, George, and was not unprepared.'

'Louisa appears to have known more of everything than I guessed,' said Onslow.

Almost as soon as he arrived, Primrose had been told about the quarrel by both the Onslows. Since then he had acted as a go-between, and had brought them to the point where they no longer slept in separate bedrooms to the wonder of the servants, but still did not speak of anything other than trivialities except through him. This situation had lasted for five days now.

'One other thing,' said Primrose, sitting down. 'Do you remember Mr Shotover, who used to be a Fellow when we were first up at Trinity? He has died, I had a letter today from his daughter, so his deanery is vacant – that of Launceston.'

'And then the bishopric of Shrewsbury is also vacant,' said Onslow heavily.

'I think it more likely you will be offered a deanery than a bishopric with Lord Palmerston in office again, you know how anxious he is to appoint evangelicals, though when I consider the nature of his private life – .' Quickly Primrose stopped himself, flushed and looked at the floor with pinched lips.

'It is Lord Shaftesbury's influence.'

'Yes, of course.'

'I have taken particular care never to seem too much the high churchman,' said Onslow. 'No one save you knows that I was a Tractarian in my youth, since I was so discreet for our old master's sake – and after all, if anyone did know, why should it be held against me now that I have so modified my views?' He spoke just as he would have done had he been able to accept the bishopric.

'You have preached several sermons on apostolic succession, George, and when you condemned the riots at St George in the East you did not make it clear that you deplored the practices there. You may not be conspicuously high nowadays, but no one could describe you as either low or broad.'

'My dear Martin, you know as well as I do that nowadays it is wholly acceptable for clergymen of all persuasions to accept the doctrine of apostolic succession, things have changed since our youth. And it is quite unnecessary to dwell on the papistical follies of St George's when denouncing the rioters.' He paused, and smiled slightly. 'In short,

142

I do not despair of being obliged to decline Shrewsbury. Remember how I denounced confession when I last preached in Westminster Abbey!'

There was another consideration which made it likely that the bishopric of Shrewsbury would be offered to him: the fact that Lord Palmerston liked him personally. He and Onslow had met twice, and on both occasions Onslow had succeeded in making him laugh. Onslow sat now looking at the books on his desk, remembering the glittering dinner at which he had first been introduced to Palmerston, thinking: no self-pity.

'Dear George,' said Primrose, who saw the pain he was in.

In all his mild life, he had never guessed that men could do such things as Onslow had done, and he wondered at it very much. Like Louisa, he was secretly more puzzled than horrified by the lusts of Onslow, though he had been distressed to learn that Onslow had any weaknesses at all, apart from his tendency to deviate from Dr Arnold's religious teachings. Primrose thought that he had never once sat in judgement on a sinner, but doing what he could to help the sinners who came his way was, for all his sorrow at their deeds, his greatest excitement and emotional interest. This did not trouble his conscience, even after his dearest friend had proved himself to be the most fascinatingly endangered of the fallen, in the worldly sphere if not in God's eyes.

'You have never told me what you think of Dr Anstey-Ward's demands, Martin,' said Onslow, pulling his chair a few inches nearer Primrose's. 'Do you think he is right? Or wrong? You have said nothing, either way, though you have done so much for me – so much I can never express my gratitude.'

There was what seemed to Onslow a long silence. Then Primrose said:

'I have been cowardly. I ought to have told you. I believe he is in the right, George, though I could wish he were less – .'

'So,' said Onslow. He whitened, for he had not realised

143

till this moment how much he relied upon Primrose to tell him that he was the victim of Mrs Grundy, not justice. 'So, sins of the flesh are unpardonable in a clergyman, as our upright atheist maintains? I am a hypocrite?'

'No,' said Primrose.

'Then?'

'It is not that you have, er, lusted, or been to an extent a hypocrite,' said Primrose. 'Good gracious no, for of whom could that not be said?'

Of you, thought Onslow, but he said nothing.

'It is that you – you have misused your authority, the power given to you.'

Unlike Anstey-Ward, who had been chiefly disgusted by the hypocrisy of Onslow, Primrose had seen this point at once – as soon as he read Onslow's letter, which showed penitence for everything but that. Onslow now stared at him with incomprehension.

'Are you implying that I have been guilty of using force?'

'No, no,' said Primrose.

'I can assure you it was far otherwise. Do not tell me either that they were too young to know what it was they did. Not one of them was a child. Not one of them was less than sixteen years old.'

'But you were still their headmaster, George.'

'I loved them,' said Onslow, thinking only of Bright.

'I do not doubt it,' said Primrose, 'but it was nonetheless wrong. There. I am honest with you. You asked me to judge, and I – '

'Oh, God,' said Onslow. 'God help me.'

Primrose leant forward. 'In your heart, don't you know that? Don't you know that you ought to have resigned your post if you could not resist temptation, instead of revelling in it? George, I would never say this to you if you were not my friend, and the man whom I shall always respect more than all others living. Don't you know, underneath, that you ought not now to hold a position of authority in the church?'

'No!' said Onslow: yet before Anstey-Ward's letter came, and even before Primrose had agreed to support him, he had made himself miserable over this possibility. It was being discovered which had killed the conscience that tortured him.

Primrose was far more shocked by Onslow's negative than he had been by the first revelation of his behaviour.

'Your letter to me was penitent,' he said, settling back in his chair. His voice was not cold, but wounded. 'Though it is hardly before me that you ought to appear penitent.'

'I do not deny that I have sinned. I say only that I have sinned no more greatly than some who now sit on the bench of bishops.'

He was thinking of a story which had made the rounds of the London clubs, and which had not come to Primrose's ears. It was a funny story, and Onslow's lips twitched as he thought of it.

A certain bishop was keeping his mistress in lodgings in the town where he had his palace. One day, she happened to mention that she had never been confirmed. Her lover, deeply shocked, persuaded her that she would be in danger of hell-fire if this ceremony continued to be neglected. He proceeded to prepare her for confirmation during his visits, before or perhaps after attending to other matters, and finally confirmed her with his own hands in the cathedral. After that, his conscience was said to have left him in peace.

Not everyone thought this story amusing, and some, thought Onslow, appeared to believe that the humour lay in the fact of a bishop's having a mistress. Their laughs were those of children first learning that adults are not what they make themselves out to be, who would think foul details more amusing than all the delicate ridiculousness in the world. Onslow remembered how he had once repeated the story to a small circle of men whom he knew not to be like that, in a soft deadpan voice. He had told it extremely well, though he had made sure he did not tell it in such a way as would make his audience think he excused the bishop's conduct.

His thoughts returned to his own deed, which included kissing boys after confirmation classes. He wondered why it was that punishment had not led him to sincere and

145

useful repentance as all punishment was supposed to do, and why, even if Anstey-Ward had been a Christian, he would have thought he was suffering unjustly. Not even Primrose's remarks could make him believe that he had sinned too greatly to be a bishop, because his sins were in the past. He had not touched a boy since Bright left Charton – but before others thought fit to judge me, thought Onslow wearily, that consideration did not lessen my internal pain, did not banish my conscience's picture of Dr Arnold and God behind him.

Intellectually, he did repent of his old sins, but he could no longer feel. It was not the kind of agonised repentance which his mother, waiting throughout his childhood for the Evangelical 'conversion' of his heart from that of a lost one into that of one saved, would have approved. And neither she nor Dr Arnold would have approved of the spurts of emotional repentance he had sometimes felt in the years before Anstey-Ward's letter came, because so far from leading to action, they had been crushed by him as he strove to cling to his sin.

He turned his mind away from this question, and made an effort to understand what Primrose had said about the abuse of power and authority.

'I know,' he said, 'that I have set the worst possible example to those boys who were the recipients of my affections. Is it for that you consider I am rightly forbidden to enjoy a bishopric?'

'No – not precisely. My meaning is rather that they could not have been able to – to consent to do as you wished altogether freely, George, and therefore you – you must be partially guilty of their error as well as your own.' He hurried on: 'Master and pupil are too unequal in possession of wisdom and of – of powers of influence. So the case is that you – why will you force me to say what will hurt you? – you have not merely, er, lusted, you have seduced, and I do think, that in a clergyman with authority over others – .' He finished: 'George, I never knew before that you felt no real regret for what you have done!'

'Good heavens!' said Onslow, ignoring this. 'And are not

146

all human beings unequal in wisdom and powers of influence? According to your logic, relations between men and women are monstrous corruption, for the difference between master and pupils is as nothing in comparison with that between man and woman!'

23

Term began to draw to a close, and as it did so, the rigid form of life at Charton started to dissolve. Lessons were learned in a perfunctory manner even by good pupils. Boys talked of what they were to do in the holidays, and of arrangements for next term, and were less unkind to each other than usual. Lovers promised to write to each other. Those who were to leave the school said farewell to Onslow and received their leaving-presents, while Onslow himself received from the Sixth Form an edition of the Aeneid, bound in vellum, as a token of their respect. Those who were to stay speculated about the new headmaster, who was not yet chosen, and wondered whether he would be more strict than Onslow.

August 11th, 1859, was the last day of term, and on that day, at a special morning service, Onslow preached his farewell sermon. While outside the chapel sweating porters struggled with boys' trunks, he preached on the subject of loneliness to an audience of pupils, former pupils, and parents. The carriages of boys' parents wanting to attend the service had inundated the village of Charton Underhill, for Onslow was a much admired headmaster, and had been recommended by *The Times* for the bishopric of Shrewsbury almost as soon as the news of his surprising resignation was made public.

Mounting the pulpit, Onslow said to his mixed congregation:

'My text is taken from the Book of Isaiah, chapter fifty-three, verse three – "I have trodden the winepress alone".' Then he paused, and massaged the sides of the pulpit with his hands. 'Brethren,' he said, 'in this morning's second lesson you heard the well-known history of our Saviour's sufferings. In the light of my chosen text, I wonder whether you have stopped to think that perhaps the chief among them was His loneliness. Remember His cry from the cross: *My God, my God, why hast Thou forsaken me?* At that hour God seemed to have forsaken Him, and man had done so. His own disciples forsook him and fled. In that hour He tasted the fullness of solitude towards both God and man. But was loneliness not the greatest of His sorrows throughout His earthly life? Was He not always alone – most of all when the multitude crowded round Him, but also in the society of the chosen few whom He condescended to call His friends? Truly, He trod the winepress alone.'

Onslow saw a father at the back nodding sagely. 'And so must we sometimes do so. I wonder how often you have thought what it means to be alone?' he said, leaning forward. 'Perhaps you may think that solitude is a great good. In youth you know little of it, and in manhood too you may lead a very busy life, and thus be glad of those rare moments when you are able to be alone, able to refresh your minds in peace. Yet this solitude which is voluntary and occasional is but half solitude. Solitude which we can exchange at will for the society which we love is a widely different thing from that solitude which is either the consequence of bereavement, or the punishment of a crime, or the result of a protracted illness. From the second solitude a merciful Providence has yet kept you, but of the first and third some among you may know something. Some among you may have suffered the bitter sorrow of bereavement. Others may at some time have been confined to a sickroom, where you have been almost as much cut off from the companions of school as from the more tender solaces of a loving home. At such times have you not felt a heavy demand made upon your cheerfulness? Have you not found disagreeable reflections and painful forebodings more likely to occupy your mind than visions of hope and thoughts of thankfulness?

149

'Then there are those among you who have returned here today from the outer world, who, I am sure, have experienced at times the sudden sense of isolation and even desolation which may come to a man when he finds himself alone in his lodging, his chambers, his college rooms, with no one to share with him the pleasures and trials of life. In such circumstances a young man, for all his love of new independence, may feel he would give the world to be once more the object of care and affection to others around and above him. And if this can be, how hard is the lot of the man who must leave his very country in the pursuit of fortune or at the call of duty! What a sense of loneliness he must have – the loneliness, if not precisely of solitude, yet of separation, of severance, of isolation! He will surely retain a lifelong recollection of that moment when the last farewells have been exchanged and the removal of the gangway has finally separated the going from the staying. What an impression he will have then of the religious trial of solitude, which reveals what manner of spirit we have, reveals to us whether we have any vitality in ourselves, or are only the creatures of society and circumstance. Yes, some of you may one day know how hard it is to remove ourselves from familiar surroundings and face a new life in solitude.'

Onslow paused again. He had decided not to refer directly to his leaving Charton, but he hoped his audience had taken the point – it seemed to him that a lady on his left was smiling encouragement.

'And,' he said gently, his voice descending the scale, 'there is the loneliness of sorrow. Is it not the feeling of loneliness which gives its sting to bereavement? In the terrible loss of a sister or a mother, a wife or a husband, is not the heart's loneliness the heaviest and bitterest part of the sorrow?

'But none of these is the most painful form of solitude. More painful by far is the loneliness of sin: not sin committed, for too often we have companions in sin, but sin felt in our hearts. For sin by its very nature separates us from God, who is present in the sickroom, in the prison,

150

in far countries, and even in bereavement. And yet despite this, when the sense of sin is upon us, then God must be our one refuge. And He is so, if we will only repent. At such times we must seek to be alone with God. No other man can help us – by the sense of sin we are separated from the world about us, and cast upon the bosom of our almighty Father.

'Such is the loneliness of repentance, but what must be the loneliness of remorse, which is repentance without God, without Christ, and therefore without hope? If repentance is loneliness, remorse is desolation. Repentance makes us lonely towards man, remorse makes us desolate towards God. That is indeed to be alone, when (to use the inspired figure) not only earth is iron, but also heaven brass. From such loneliness may God in His mercy save us all through His Son Jesus Christ.'

Onslow spoke these words clearly, but inwardly he was in turmoil. When writing the sermon yesterday, he had been perfectly calm, and had not consciously applied it to his own case, his own sense of sin. But hearing his own voice he did so now. He struggled on to his next paragraph, but the struggle was not visible to his audience.

'I have spoken of loneliness through which we shall probably all pass, before we leave the world. But there remain one or two through which we must undoubtedly all pass, whatever we are.

'There is the loneliness of death. In death we shall be alone, and shall feel ourselves to be so. Friends may be around us, they will not be with us. The soul is already alone with God, viewing itself as in His sight, and pre- paring for a yet closer access. The words of a Christian friend may suggest thoughts of solemnity or hope; his prayers may encourage, comfort, and help us; but he is no longer with us as he once was.' Onslow thought of Prim- rose, who was sitting at the back of the chapel.

'Can we then follow the soul one step further, and see it standing in judgement before the throne of God? At that moment we shall be alone, alone for the last time before we enter forever into the society of the good or the evil. In the

151

one case, there is no such thing as a separate existence because all are gathered together and lost in God – while in the other there can be no separate existence because evil is at last gathered to its kind. Not for sympathy, for there can be no sympathy, amongst the evil, but for the mutual repulsion and unceasing discord which is everywhere where God is not. That discord and repulsion may be regarded as one half of the future punishment which awaits the despisers of an offered mercy in another world.' Onslow gripped the pulpit and went on a little more loudly than before, seeing that some of those beneath him were looking as unhappy as he felt.

'If you are to die alone, and if you are to be judged alone, be not afraid to think alone, and to pray alone, and if necessary to act alone. What good will it do any of us to have had a whole multitude with us in doing wrong? for the beloved company of others is all too often an evil influence. What will that excuse be worth at a judgement seat before which we are standing alone – the excuse that others said so, that everyone did so? That is not the question. The question is was it right to do so? was your conscience satisfied that it was right to do so? My brethren, we would not be such servile followers of one another if we could only realise and remember the fact that we must stand alone before God. Far better to be singular now than to be condemned then, far better to face God alone now in prayer, however difficult it may be, than to incur the wrath of Him who is able to destroy soul and body in Hell.

'Perhaps the view of life I have presented to you seems dreary, even grim,' he said to the bowed heads of some of his pupils, whom he would never see again. 'Yet let any who think so remember that though we must pray and think alone, and die and be judged alone, there is still a reality of sympathy which we may find and rejoice in if we wish. It is a sympathy unchangeable and eternal, sympathy with Him who so loved us that He died for us, and who is the same yesterday and today and forever. My brethren, He is with us in all our lonely trials, and He will save us, if we will but hearken to His voice within us.'

152

As he spoke these words, Onslow came close to tears. He raised his head proudly. Looking down at those below him, nearly all of whom he supposed would side with Anstey-Ward, he thought: yes, I still have Thee. Thou art with me. Thou wilt extend Thy mercy to a sinner who has repented. Lord, now permit Thy servant to depart in peace!

24

When it became known that Dr Onslow of Charton had
turned down both the bishopric of Shrewsbury and the
deanery of Launceston, and wished to spend the rest of his
life in the obscurity of a country parsonage, considerable
astonishment was felt by the many people who had never
suspected him of undue humility. Some of them wondered whether anything could be behind it, but for the
most part they concluded that surprising though it was,
Onslow was struggling with the demon of worldly
ambition, which most clergymen in his position would
never have recognised, let alone fought. Onslow allowed
this to be known: he told one person that he was indeed
afraid of ambition, and waited for the news to spread. He
became an even more highly respected figure than he used
to be, and was soon offered the choice of three suitable
livings. One was in Surrey, one in Devon, and one, by a
slender margin the most generously endowed, was in
Derbyshire. He chose the Derbyshire rectory, though
Louisa, who had never been north of Warwick in her life,
wanted the Surrey vicarage in spite of the fact that it was
worth only six hundred a year. She believed it would be a
comfort to both of them to be close to London and Primrose
in their poverty, but, perversely she thought, Onslow opted
for the more absolute exile of Hinterton in Derbyshire. It
was almost as though he really were fighting an internal
demon of worldly ambition.

Hinterton was situated four miles north of Ashbourne,
in the southern foothills of the Pennine Chain, and the
surrounding countryside was in a bleak way very beautiful.

154

The village was built round a crossroads. It consisted of some forty cottages, a public house, a small shop, a church, and three gentlemen's houses including the rectory. It resembled Charton in that it was built on a slope, and from the rectory and church at the top of the gentle hill it was possible to look down and see the descending row of houses which formed the main street, just as it had been possible at Charton to look down from the railway station and see the builded fruits of Onslow's activity.

The Onslows moved into the rectory late in November, 1859. They furnished it almost exactly as they had furnished Charton, and then, settled at last, they looked out from it into the unchanging future. At Hinterton, they had the peace for which Onslow had asked God when he preached for the last time in the school chapel.

======

One afternoon in February 1860, Louisa was entertaining the wife of the rector of Tudbury, a parish which lay south of Ashbourne. She had not met the woman before. Mrs Lucas's ninth pregnancy and the subsequent childbirth had kept her at home while the rest of the neighbouring clergy and gentry were making the acquaintance of the Onslows. Now Mrs Lucas was hastening to make up for lost time. She asked good-humoured questions as though she had known Louisa for years.

'Do you not find us very dull, after Charton, Mrs Onslow?'

'What can I possibly say to that?' said Louisa, smiling a little. She was soberly dressed today, as she always was now, and she had aged a little since the summer. She was thinner, and her cheeks were hollow.

'Very true!' said Mrs Lucas. 'What a foolish question to ask – pray forget it.'

Louisa did not choose to forget it. She said seriously:

'I do not think Dr Onslow finds it dull, or at all events a little comparative dullness has been what he was looking

155

for. And as for me' – she hesitated – 'I assure you, I am enjoying my new surroundings very much.'

'I am sure Dr Onslow must be quite worn out after fifteen years, was it, of caring for naughty boys.'

'Oh, quite so.'

There was a pause.

'Do you plan to make many changes in the parish?' said Mrs Lucas, who had already heard of certain changes from her husband, who was the rural dean.

'Dr Onslow has instituted monthly communion. And he is planning to take up the box pews in the church. I hope no one will think ill of him for that,' said Louisa.

'Villagers are so conservative. But for my part I think it is an excellent scheme to remove those old pews. Horrid things, like great bathing-machines! Mr Lucas removed them at Tudbury when he first came.'

'I am glad you approve. I hope all our neighbours will do so.'

'Oh, they will! Mr Johnson was so very set in his ways, very old-fashioned. Not even a Sunday school! Of course he had no wife to help him.'

'Something must be done about that,' said Louisa. 'But I have no experience of setting up schools. I daresay I shall contrive.'

Mrs Lucas laughed.

'Oh Mrs Onslow, you and Dr Onslow surely cannot say you have no experience of schools!'

'But there is a difference,' said Louisa, 'between Charton and a Sunday school for labourers' children.'

'So there is!' Mrs Lucas seemed to think Louisa had made a joke. She glanced at the clock on the drawing-room mantelpiece, and saw that she had already stayed a little longer than was proper on a first call. Getting to her feet, she said:

'I must take my leave of you, Mrs Onslow. But first, do you and Dr Onslow care to dine with us on Wednesday of next week? Mr Lucas and I are giving a dinner-party, and my father is coming to it. He lives in Italy, you know, and

156

rarely visits England, but I know he will be most interested to meet Dr Onslow.'

Mrs Lucas's father was Lord Burnam, the owner of Tudbury. Louisa already knew this, though she was not yet a person with whom her new neighbours would gossip about Lord Burnam's loose manner of living.

'I think we shall be delighted, Mrs Lucas.'

Louisa thought of how everyone was most interested to meet Dr Onslow. She and her husband had enjoyed quite a little social life since coming to Hinterton, among those whose faces would soon grow as familiar as the view from the rectory drawing-room had already become. Few of them were disagreeable people, but no more could be said of them by the Onslows. None of the clergymen in the district was either a notable scholar or connected with the higher reaches of the church, and most of the lay people whom they had met were chiefly interested in hunting. But all these neighbours were curious to know why such a rising star as Onslow had chosen to fall to earth among them, just as a few months earlier, the Onslows' old acquaintance had been astonished by their retirement.

When Mrs Lucas was gone, Louisa took out her embroidery. She would work at it solidly till dinner-time. There was nothing else to do, and Louisa, as she worked at it, forgot that at Charton too she had had many empty hours. The emptiness felt quite different now, because her husband, who had had little free time in the old days, was now almost as leisured as she was, and this somehow emphasised her own boredom.

———

The parish of Hinterton had been run by a curate for the past five years, ever since the Onslows' predecessor became too infirm for his duties. Onslow had not dispensed with this curate's services, though he told himself he ought to, in order to give himself more to do and thus distract his mind. But he did not, for it was with difficulty that he forced himself to do anything at all, even on Sundays. Only

157

pride made him act, as he had done in instituting monthly communion, and in deciding to remove the old box pews from the village church. These acts, he knew, were such as would be expected of him.

There was one duty of a clergyman which Onslow longed to shirk, but felt he could not altogether even though he had a diligent curate: visiting his poorer parishioners in their homes.

On the day Mrs Lucas called on Louisa, Onslow made himself go down to the other end of the village to visit a family called Roberts. Their cottage was one of the most unpleasant in the locality: a little, old building with two tiny rooms upstairs and one small room down, and in this lived a family of seven, including a grandfather who was gradually dying. When Onslow entered the cottage after knocking at the door he was assailed by the smell of humanity and of cabbage – Mrs Roberts had been stirring a black pot suspended by chains over an open fire. A baby was crawling near the hearth, a three year old and a five year old were sitting at a battered, stained deal table. The last two stared at Onslow as their mother ushered him in.

'Mrs Roberts, is it not? I hope I have not come to call on you at an inconvenient time.'

'Oh no, sir,' she replied, taking off her apron as she spoke. Mrs Roberts, having been in service, did not speak with quite so thick a Derbyshire accent as some of the villagers.

'It is my wish to make the acquaintance of all my parishioners,' said Onslow. The curate had told him that the Roberts family did not attend church regularly; neither did they visit the dissenting chapel. They were merely indifferent. Onslow supposed that perhaps, as a priest, he ought to seek to remedy this, yet he felt he could not question the woman about her churchgoing, not yet. At one moment he felt that to do so would be almost a kind of impertinence, at the next that it was hard to believe that a woman in her circumstances was a human soul in need of priestly care. He wondered what to say, and remembered how he had never been at a loss for words in his old life, in which he had never spoken to a poor person.

'I hope I find you in good health?' he said, as Mrs Roberts dusted the seat of a chair and offered it to him.

'A'm middling, thank you sir.'

'Good!' said Onslow. 'And your children – what a fine little fellow this baby is.' The baby had crawled to his feet. Its face was very dirty.

'Aye, he's well enough.'

'Do you go on prosperously? Is your pig well?' Onslow had learnt from the curate that the villagers' pigs, kept in sties behind the cottages, were very important to them, being their only source of meat.

'He's not very clever just now, the pig.'

'I am sorry to hear that,' said Onslow. 'Your husband is a shepherd, I believe, Mrs Roberts?'

'Aye, he is.'

'I hope he is well?' Onslow had never felt so foolish in his life.

'Aye, sir.'

'Have you other children besides these I see?'

'Oh aye, sir. A've seven all told.'

'At work in the fields with their father, I presume? Are your older girls in service?'

'Aye, our Polly went into service in the back-end.'

'How old is she?' said Onslow, who thought that the back-end meant not the autumn, but some unknown place.

'Twelve, sir.'

'Twelve. She is your eldest?'

'Aye, sir.'

'Is her place in service far from here?' he said.

'Oh no. In Wirksworth.'

'It must be agreeable to have her so close.'

'Oh, it is sir.'

Wearily Onslow thought of the struggle it would be to write a sermon suitable for the ears of Mrs Roberts. It was a task he found impossible, he had not even attempted it. Since coming to Hinterton he had preached his old Charton sermons, with minor variations, to a congregation which

159

contained hardly anyone capable of understanding them but the local squire and his family.

'I believe Mrs Onslow brought some calves'-foot jelly for your father-in-law, Mrs Roberts.'

'Aye, three days since. We're grateful, sir.'

'Is your father-in-law a little improved?'

'Not to speak of, sir.'

'Would he care to have me visit him?'

'Oh yes, I'm sure.'

'Good, good.'

'Shall I take you upstairs, sir?'

'If you will be so good.'

Mrs Roberts led the way up the narrow, rickety staircase, and opened the door of a frowsty little room. Onslow stepped in, and looked at a bed heaped with clothes, inside which there was an old, slack-mouthed man. He supposed he would have to ask the old man whether anything was troubling his spirit, as was surely likely now he was close to death. The conscience, Onslow thought, must become active at such a time even in an unbeliever.

He could only wish that he were close to death himself, and not likely to spend more than thirty years in making visits of this kind, pretending to be a better, humbler Christian than he was or ever would be.

25

The squire of Hinterton was a Mr Butterick, a pleasant, cultivated man of fifty. He was delighted to have so distinguished a man as Onslow for the rector of the parish, and soon became friendly with him. As for the Onslows, to them Mr Butterick's presence in the neighbourhood seemed a species of blessing, for at Hinterton, the presence of any man familiar with the *Iliad* would have appeared so.

One morning in May of 1860, when Onslow was spending his daily hour with the Bible, Mr Butterick came to call at the rectory. Onslow was glad enough to see him, glad to have the rigid routine to which he clung interrupted.

'Dr Onslow,' said the squire, after a few civilities had been exchanged, 'I will no longer conceal from you that I have come here to ask a very great favour of you.'

'Have you, sir? I am sure I shall be delighted to grant it,' said Onslow politely.

Mr Butterick took out his watch and wound it.

'It is my son Tom, who has been rusticated from Cambridge for a stupid prank. Well, boys will be boys as they say, but what chiefly concerns me is the fact that he appears to have done almost no work.'

'They never do, Mr Butterick.'

'Yes, it is all very well, but Tom has to have a profession. He cannot afford to be plucked. I have brought him to see that this cannot continue, and he works with me every morning, but the fact is that while I remember my classics tolerably well, I never was able to understand mathematics. Fortunately at Oxford that did not prevent me from taking

161

honours, but Tom was set on Cambridge – I have been wondering – '

'Perhaps you would like me to offer him a little tuition?' said Onslow.

'Dare I ask it? It is very presumptuous of me to think you might wish to spend your time in such a way, but I do not know what I am to do.'

'Certainly! I was once a Wrangler, but I am more than a trifle rusty, and shall be glad to take up my mathematics again.'

Thus a small change was introduced into Onslow's life.

===

Next day, as soon as he shook hands with him in his study, Onslow remembered having met Tom Butterick before. He wondered why the boy had made only a vague impression on him on that occasion (an evening party given by his parents at Christmas), for Tom was distinctly attractive. He had curling brown hair, bright eyes, a straight little nose, and a good figure. His appearance was spoilt only by his hands, which were like great ruddy spades.

'I hope we shall become friends, you and I,' he said.

'I hope so, sir,' replied Tom. He looked to be listless, the sort of boy whom in the old days Onslow had tried to punish into intelligence.

'I take it you are not fond of mathematics, Mr Butterick?' It seemed odd to be calling a pupil 'Mr', but Onslow remembered that he was now teaching an undergraduate, not a schoolboy. It was twenty years since as a young Fellow and tutor of Trinity, Onslow had taught undergraduates. He thought to himself that he must remember that period of his life rather than the other.

'I'm not especially fond of it, no, sir,' said Tom, and added in a voice of punctilious boredom: 'It's very good of you to offer to teach me.'

'Not at all. I see you have brought your Euclid. Perhaps you had best show me which propositions trouble you, and I will see whether I can make you understand.'

162

'Yes, sir.'

They sat down together at the study table, and their legs brushed as they did so. Tom smelt of soap, but underlying the soap smell there was something more animal – yet it did not resemble the animal smell of the villagers' cottages. Onslow, noticing this, wondered whether Tom had been forced into coming to him for lessons by threats of a reduced allowance. His somewhat sullen demeanour made this seem likely, but Onslow, though he wished it were not so, was determined not to be daunted.

The lesson did not go well. Tom turned out to be stupid, stupid at any rate where mathematics were concerned. Onslow, instead of being repelled by this, found himself longing to make the boy understand. He never used to feel like that at Charton. There, if a boy proved to be slow, he either mocked him or ignored him. But then, he thought, he had had many bright pupils to delight him, some of whom were handsomer than Tom.

As they worked together, Onslow was constantly aware of the warmth of the boy's body, constantly distracted by his touchingly sparse whiskers and the way his hair merged into down at the nape of his neck. It was nearly a year since he had been close enough to any boy to observe such details.

———

Over the course of three weeks, Tom's mathematics barely improved, and Onslow became increasingly frustrated as he sat by him day after day. It seemed to him that Tom was not altogether unintelligent, for his remarks on general subjects were sensible enough, and so he was forced to wonder whether he himself were not a bad teacher. Tom's failure to make progress gradually made him wonder whether even at Charton, teaching classics, he had really been as good a schoolmaster as he would have liked to be and had once believed he was. Unwillingly, in Tom's presence, he remembered how often he had failed to kindle interest in boys' minds – he had forgotten that since leaving, had only remembered a golden age filled with docile and

163

intelligent pupils. It was terrible to have such doubts about his past, the thought of which had in recent months been as much a comfort as a source of pain to him. It was as terrible as knowing that he could never make any move towards any boy now that he was outside the enclosed, distorted world of Charton.

One morning, Onslow told Tom to copy out several of Euclid's propositions from memory. He thought this task could not be beyond the boy. As Tom worked, Onslow stood by the open window and thought of what Primrose had said to him about his true sin being not carnal but a misuse of authority. He was beginning to understand what his friend had meant, now that he had no authority to misuse.

'I have finished, sir,' said Tom, and Onslow turned his head.

'Have you, Mr Butterick?' he said, coming over to the table. Tom handed him two sheets of paper, and Onslow put on his spectacles to inspect them.

Tom had not remembered one of the propositions correctly. Onslow raised his head and looked at his fair, unconscious face. He thought he detected a trace of smugness in the boy's expression, and quite suddenly, his feelings of frustration overcame him.

'How brilliant, how admirable is this piece of work, sir,' he said in the voice of biting sarcasm he used to use at Charton. 'Allow me only to make one or two corrections.' Grabbing Tom's quill, he drew it across the paper in a great X, so hard that he broke it. Tom, who had been treated with cool kindness by Onslow till now, could not understand what was happening.

'All I can say, sir, is that you are very fortunate that the Senate now allows men to try for classical honours without more mathematics than the Previous. In my day it was very different!' He paused and stared at Tom's face, which was one of stupid shock. 'Are your classics as poor as your mathematics? It would not surprise me to learn so.'

'Yes, sir,' said Tom after a moment, almost defiantly. He

164

was determined not to be cowed, for he was no longer a schoolboy.

'Then why are you taking honours at all?'

'Because my father refuses to let me go out in the poll. I know well enough that I would be lucky even to get a poll degree.'

Onslow sat down, and there was silence for a while. Then he said:

'My dear boy, I must apologise to you. I have been unforgivably ill-tempered.'

'Don't mention it sir, I expect I deserved all you said,' Tom replied stiffly. He thought Onslow slightly mad for having lost his temper in such a way, and he also thought that the man, having given way to his passion, was looking older than usual. It occurred to him to wonder whether Onslow was quite happy at Hinterton.

'I think I had better not come again,' he said. 'I am going back to Cambridge next week in any case.'

'But what will you tell your father?' was all Onslow could think of to say.

'I don't know.'

Onslow said: 'Would you like me to speak to him?'

'Speak to him?'

'I could, for example, tell him that you ought to be permitted to take a poll degree instead of trying for honours. If that is all I can do for you.' Onslow wanted very much to do something for Tom, to compensate not only for his loss of control but for his secret feelings.

'I don't think he would listen to you, sir. He is altogether set on my taking honours.' He added with a kind of laugh: 'He's made me work harder now than I ever did at Cambridge.'

'He is a strict parent?' Onslow would never have thought it of the polite and genial Mr Butterick.

'Yes, sir.'

'Dear me,' said Onslow, in a normal voice.

Tom hesitated, then said:

'No, perhaps I am wrong, perhaps he would listen to you. I was forgetting you were a headmaster for such a long time, sir. If you told him my abilities are not equal to my taking honours he might believe you.'

'You would like me to do that?' said Onslow.

'I think so, sir.'

'That is all I can do to make amends for my outburst?'

'I'd be very grateful, sir.'

'I fear to incur his wrath.'

The boy smiled. He could not believe this. He did not understand that it was important for Onslow to be on good terms with his father, for he lived in a wider world than Hinterton.

'But naturally I will not allow such a consideration to deter me,' said Onslow, getting up from his chair. He added: 'Yet perhaps it would be best if you did come here on Wednesday and Friday as usual, Mr Butterick. I think I might be able to make out a more convincing case if I were known to have carried on to the bitter end, if I may so phrase it.'

'Oh, I don't think so, sir,' said Tom. He meant to spend the hours he should have been with Onslow out of doors, and could only hope that no one would remark on having seen him.

'We need not devote our time to mathematics. We might discuss all manner of things – I would like to hear your account of life at Cambridge as it is now. I am sure it has changed a good deal since my day,' Onslow pleaded. He could not bear to think that he had wantonly deprived himself of another two hours of the boy's company, even though that company caused him such irritation.

'I expect it has, sir.'

'Well,' said Onslow, 'consider what I have said. In the meantime I suppose you ought to go now, or else you will be late for luncheon.'

'Yes.'

Onslow stretched out his hand and said: 'I am forgiven?'

'Oh yes. And thank you again, sir, for all you have done for me,' said Tom. He took Onslow's hand, then dropped it, then went.

Onslow felt almost as he had done two years before,

when Bright said goodbye in his study at Charton. Such, he thought, was the effect of the punishment which Anstey-Ward had no doubt thought would reform him. It had made him desperate even for the shadow of his former delights, and there was no hope of his ever feeling differently.

26

'I did not see your pupil come in today, George,' said Louisa at dinner, two days after Onslow parted from Tom Butterick. 'Is he unwell?'

'He is no longer my pupil,' said Onslow.

'Oh,' said Louisa, who had scarcely ever mentioned Tom to her husband, and by pointedly failing to do so had both relieved and frightened him.

'He and I were agreed that it would be useless to continue. I can do nothing for him.'

'I am sorry.'

Onslow hesitated, and Louisa could see that he was wondering whether to speak. She waited, and at length he said rather stiffly:

'It was not to be, but I hoped that I would be able to do as I did for many boys at Charton, or at least as I believe I did, and awaken a love of learning in him.'

'Did you hope that?'

'Why else do you suppose I agreed to give him lessons, when I learnt how things were with him?'

'Oh, out of a wish to oblige Mr Butterick,' said Louisa. 'Am I not right then?'

'I have seldom had a more obstinately stupid pupil,' Onslow told her.

'I am sorry,' said Louisa a second time. Then:

'But he is a handsome young man, is he not?'

'He is not ill-favoured, no.'

Louisa dared say no more. But however painful it would be, she wanted to hear the whole story of his feelings for Tom Butterick, and not to pretend that young boys had nothing to do with their being at Hinterton. She wanted to be intimate with her husband, whom she no longer lightly called 'Dr Onslow'. To her, the time for calling him that was past. She was too thoroughly bound to him and his faults now to feel anything other than an experienced wife, but she thought it was hard to make Onslow see that things had changed between them. He did not wish to see it, he wished to pretend that all was as it had been. Louisa guessed that even now, he could not forgive her for having known the truth.

After eating a few mouthfuls of mutton in silence, Louisa said:

'I think we ought to go away for a while. I can see that your spirits are low, and perhaps a little travelling would do them good.' She wondered whether he would rebuff her, but all he said was:

'We cannot afford to travel, Louisa. You forget that our circumstances have changed.'

'Do you indeed think I forget it?' She wondered how she could do so when every day she was made aware of the fact that they employed no male servants indoors, and kept no carriage but a gig.

'I do not mean to imply that you are extravagant.'

Onslow, inspecting the beautifully-kept household books, had almost wished that Louisa were extravagant, so that he might blame her for a small part of his unhappiness. During their time at Charton, he had had a mental picture of Louisa as an expensive little puss, though she had never once overspent her generous allowance. Now he was forced to see that his idea of her had been false.

'I am glad of that,' said Louisa dryly.

He looked at her.

'I wish we might go away for a while, indeed,' he said, to conciliate her. The last thing he wanted was a quarrel, or even a coldness – he wanted the easy, friendly relationship they had had in the past.

'Perhaps you would prefer to go alone?'

'Oh no,' said Onslow. 'On the whole I think that if I were to travel I would prefer to have you with me. I have

169

no wish to be alone.' He dreaded to think what he might do if he were alone.

'I am pleased to hear you say that. What a pity we cannot go even for a fortnight to the seaside!' She added: 'I expect we could do that, in fact, but I know you do not care for watering-places.'

Though they had effectively ruled out the possibility of travelling, a few days later the Onslows received an invitation to travel in a small way. It came from an old friend of Onslow's, Dr Powell, who had lately been made Master of one of the colleges at Oxford. He invited them to stay with him and his wife for a week or so, and told them that Primrose would be coming. The Onslows decided that this was just what they were looking for, and on the 24th of June, they left Hinterton for the first time since they arrived there the previous November. Onslow looked forward to dining at High Table much as a girl of seventeen might look forward to her presentation; Louisa thought rather of the pleasures of the Botanic Gardens.

=====

One evening after supper, when one of Dr Powell's daughters had just finished playing the piano, Primrose said to him:

'Powell, my dear fellow, I am sure you have been paying attention to this meeting of the British Association. I have a mind to attend it tomorrow – I hear it is not open to the public, but would you as a member be able to introduce me into the hall?'

'I see no reason why not,' said Dr Powell, who took a keen amateur interest in entomology. 'But why are you so interested? I had no notion that natural science was of any interest to you.'

'Oh no, not in general, but I am told that old Soapy Sam, whom I so much dislike, is proposing to demolish Mr Darwin's new theory of transmutation, which I find most impressive, most interesting – I do not know what you think of it?'

'Let us say I have grave doubts.'

'Well, I am very sure the good bishop will make a fool of himself and I long to be in at the kill, as it were.'

'How very uncharitable, Martin,' said Onslow. Primrose often talked with cheerful callousness after a glass or two of wine. 'But what is this new theory? Has not transmutation been discussed in certain circles for many years now?' He thought of Anstey-Ward.

Another man, a young scientist, spoke before Primrose could reply.

'If you are hoping that the Bishop will make a fool of himself you probably hope in vain, Mr Primrose. He has consulted leading authorities in the field, Professor Owen in particular. He will not be arguing purely as a bigot, and for my part, though I don't absolutely say that Mr Darwin is wrong, I think Professor Owen's objections to his book are well founded.'

'Are they? Of course, I do not know about that,' said Primrose. He turned to Onslow, and briefly described *The Origin of Species*, which had appeared the previous November and escaped Onslow's attention. The book was not yet a matter of public concern, though it had sold well for a scientific work.

'I do not know how you can talk about such a thing so light-heartedly,' said Onslow in disgust.

'Now come, George, you are as prepared as the next man to own that all too much of what we were taught in childhood was not literal truth. How is this different?'

'Do you not see that this or any other idea of transmutation would abolish any notion of design, of final cause? It is not a mere detail, like the Flood. How can it possibly be compatible with religious truth – with an omniscient Deity?'

'Why, it does not diminish God's glory in the least,' said Primrose, surprised. 'Don't you see it is no less glorious, miraculous even, for Him to have set so astonishing a – a mechanism in motion, than for Him to have ordered special creations?'

The young scientist listened to the clergymen's argument with a sardonic look on his face. Primrose's ignorant enthusiasm for Darwin's book was more responsible for this than Onslow's intransigence: it made him wonder what the Church was coming to.

'No, I do not,' said Onslow. 'You are worshipping the repulsive God of the Deists of the last century, Martin, not a Person, if that is what you think.'

'How interesting it will be to hear the debate on this subject!' said Mrs Powell, who disliked argument in her drawing-room. Louisa was grateful for her interruption: her old dread of a quarrel between Onslow and Primrose had been revived by their interchange. 'Tell me, who is to reply to the bishop? Is it Mr Darwin himself?'

'No, he is by far too unwell, so I have heard,' said her husband. 'He will not be present at all. I believe that if anyone replies it will be Sir Joseph Hooker.'

'Mr Huxley?' suggested the young scientist.

'Possibly, but he seems somewhat unwilling to champion Mr Darwin in public. You were not present at yesterday's meeting? He had very little to say – merely remarked that a general audience was not one in front of which he could expatiate. And when Professor Owen observed that the brain of the highest ape bears no more resemblance to that of man than does that of any other creature, all he could produce was a flat denial.'

'Who is Mr Huxley?' said Primrose.

'Oh, a naturalist, not a man of any great note in the world of science. One odd circumstance is that he looks remarkably like a Wilberforce, so like that he could almost be the bishop's son,' said Dr Powell.

'How odd, to be sure!' said Mrs Powell.

'I think I would like to attend this meeting also,' said Onslow, for whom the subject of transmutation was like a loose tooth to be painfully waggled. 'Could it be arranged, Powell?'

'Why, I believe so. Mrs Onslow, would you care to join us?'

'Oh yes,' said Louisa, who had nothing better to do.

Thus it was settled that theirs would be a party of five: the Powells, the Onslows, and Primrose, who was the only person to regard Mr Darwin's theory with positive favour.

27

The next afternoon, Dr Powell and his party went along to the hall where the meeting was to take place. It was a larger hall than the one which had served the members of the British Association till that Saturday, and had been chosen at the last moment, for so many people wished to hear Bishop Wilberforce that the old hall could not contain them. There were over seven hundred present in all, including noisy undergraduates and ladies in billowing bright dresses, but the majority of those who had come to listen were members of the Association.

'Gracious me, what a crush,' said Louisa as they pushed their way through towards a row of empty seats. It was not so very bad, but her crinoline was making it difficult for her to move, and seriously inconveniencing those she passed.

'Yes, indeed,' said Primrose. 'But here we are.'

As they prepared to sit down, Onslow noticed that a man seated some feet away was looking intently in their direction: then he saw that it was Anstey-Ward. For a moment the two men stared at each other. Slowly, Anstey-Ward gave a kind of half salute, to which Onslow replied with the hint of a bow. Then Louisa, observing this, also recognised Anstey-Ward. She gave a gasp of surprise as he raised his hat to her.

'Who is that man, Louie?' said Primrose.

'It's Dr Anstey-Ward.'

'Indeed!'

'Yes. I believe he must be a member of the Association –

his house as I remember was full of rocks and dead animals.'

Onslow began to talk about the Bishop.

'I can only imagine that Soapy Sam is attempting to restore his family's reputation. When two of one's brothers have gone over to Rome, it is desirable to make it quite clear that one remains such a sound Low Churchman as one's father would have approved. I can only hope he does not carry it too far.'

In contrast Anstey-Ward, like Primrose, was hoping that the Bishop would make a fool of himself – though he supposed there was not much chance of that, for he knew that both Sir Joseph Hooker and Mr Huxley expected him to be a formidable opponent.

Having acknowledged Onslow's presence, Anstey-Ward took out his watch and wound it, though it did not need winding. As he did so he thought that he ought not to be so very surprised at the Onslows being here. The room was full of women and clergymen, even though the meeting was not officially open to the public. And it was quite possible and allowable for Onslow to come down occasionally from his northern fastness.

Anstey-Ward had been almost as impressed as Primrose by *The Origin of Species*, but it worried him, as it had done with earlier theories of transmutation, that the fossil record provided so little which could be called evidence in favour of the hypothesis. Now he forgot this worry: he remembered the interview he had had eleven months ago with Onslow in his library, and he became a determined, instead of a moderate, supporter of Darwin. He had no doubts what Onslow was thinking. Neither had Onslow about the thoughts of Anstey-Ward.

A hush descended: the speakers had begun to arrive and make their way towards the platform.

The proceedings began with the reading of a paper by a Dr John William Draper, the title of which was 'The Intellectual Development of Europe with reference to the views of Mr Darwin'. Dr Draper was an admirer of Darwin, and in his hour-long speech he drew parallels between the

174

gradual upward development of species and the progress of the human intellect towards enlightenment. Few people in the audience were interested in his views, for the majority of listeners regarded the expression of them as a tiresome preliminary to the bishop's speech, while the professional scientists in the audience thought them wholly irrelevant to the real issue. But Anstey-Ward and Onslow listened intently, and were agreed that the paper consisted largely of crass generalisations. Onslow was delighted.

'Well, I am glad that has come to an end at last,' said Mrs Powell, fanning herself with a piece of paper. 'Are we now to hear the bishop?'

'Presently, my dear,' said her husband, who saw quite a different man rise to begin the discussion. The man was an economist, and he objected to Darwin's views on religious grounds, but he was not allowed to develop his ideas, for the undergraduates grouped in one part of the hall shouted him down in their impatience for Bishop Wilberforce. They treated the next speaker similarly, but this had nothing to do with their being in favour of Darwin, for when a third man rose to say something, this time in Darwin's defence, they behaved in just the same way. The speaker wished to give a mathematical demonstration of the truth of Darwin's views, and drew a diagram on a blackboard, saying: 'Let this point A be man, and let that point B be the monkey'. He pronounced 'monkey' as 'mawnkey', and this gave the undergraduates the opportunity to yell: 'Mawnkey! Mawnkey!'

The chairman of the meeting tried to keep order, but to no avail. The audience would be satisfied with nothing less than the bishop.

'How shockingly all these young men are behaving,' said Louisa, who had a certain sympathy for them.

'Yes,' said Onslow, 'and I see that some of them are former Charton boys.'

On the platform, a professor rose to ask for a fair hearing, and then at last, Bishop Wilberforce took the floor.

His speech was a sweetly-phrased mockery of Darwin's work and its supporters, referring to 'our unsuspected cousinship with the mushrooms'. 'Is it credible,' he asked, 'that all favourable varieties of turnip are tending to become men, and yet that the closest microscopic observation has never detected the faintest tendency in the highest of the Algae to improve into the very lowest Zoophyte?' The Onslows approved of this, but Anstey-Ward and Primrose thought it inaccurate and unfair.

Having described Professor Owen's scientific objections to the theory of evolution, the bishop made an objection of his own: he asked whether woman, as well as man, could possibly be descended from an ape. The ladies in the audience were for the most part well pleased by this gallantry. Some waved their handkerchiefs in token of appreciation. Then the bishop turned to Mr Huxley and said:

'Is it through his grandmother or his grandfather that Mr Huxley claims descent from a monkey?'

At this there was laughter from many people. Onslow sucked in his cheeks, while Anstey-Ward reddened with anger at the frivolity of the question.

Mr Huxley did not reply, merely whispered something to his neighbour, and the bishop wound up with a fluent denunciation of Darwin's theory as plainly contrary to scripture. He insisted that it was not only incompatible with the revealed Word of God, but also with God's works and spirit: incompatible with Man's supremacy on earth, with his gift of reason, with the Incarnation of God's Son. And if Mr Darwin's theories were to be believed, Man would sink into brutish sensuality. These remarks, thought Anstey-Ward, proved Wilberforce to be a mere bigot, a man like Onslow. Onslow, for his part, thought the bishop had made a mistake in appealing directly to the revealed Word and to theological reasoning. He believed he ought rather to have clung to scientific arguments which were compatible with revelation, for to do otherwise was to bring a great Voltairean axe down between religion and reason, and damage the unity of truth.

When the bishop had finished, the delighted audience called for a reply to his speech, and Mr Huxley finally got to his feet. Anstey-Ward and Onslow watched him keenly as he spoke, beginning with a simple defence of evolution as a legitimate hypothesis. He admitted that Mr Darwin had not proved that natural selection did in fact operate to produce new species, but insisted that he had proved all that was provable. The hypothesis agreed with all available facts, and explained many things which had hitherto been puzzling. Next he explained that there was no question of man's being descended from the ape, but only a question of both ape and man being descended from a remote common ancestor. And then Mr Huxley turned to the remarks about his own ancestry which had won the bishop such applause. Fixing his eyes on him, he said:

'A man has no reason to be ashamed of having an ape for his grandfather. If there were an ancestor whom I should feel shame in recalling, it would rather be a man, a man of restless and versatile intellect, who, not content with equivocal success in his own sphere of activity, plunges into scientific questions with which he has no real acquaintance, only to obscure them by an aimless rhetoric, and distract the attention of his hearers from the real point at issue by eloquent digressions and skilled appeals to religious prejudice.'

There was uproar in the hall. No one had expected the bishop to be denounced so plainly, and in his own diocese at that. One lady swooned with shock at the crude words 'religious prejudice', and was carried out. Out of nerves, Louisa giggled as she had done at the bishop's remark about Mr Huxley's grandmother; while Anstey-Ward, Onslow saw, looked grimly satisfied. He wished he could tell the man that his champion had met wit with mere rudeness, and that the bishop remained in the right – yet all the while, he knew that Mr Huxley's reply had been a good one.

The meeting was not over. When Mr Huxley was finished, an Oxford don rose and told the audience that the theory of upward development could not be true, because Homer had lived three thousand years ago and his like had not been seen since. Anstey-Ward was pleased by the

177

foolishness of this, thinking that if no better argument could be found by Darwin's opponents, the day was won. He was pleased even though many in the audience did not seem to perceive the folly of the don's observation. Some of them appeared not to have heard at all: there was still a good deal of noise and confusion in the hall.

Then, speaking as a partisan of Darwin, Sir John Lubbock sought to expose some of the frauds which had been perpetrated with the aim of discrediting theories of development. He instanced a grain of wheat which had been supposed to have come from a mummy's tomb in Egypt. He had been told that this single grain showed that wheat had not changed since the time of the Pharaohs – but the wheat, he said, had turned out to be made of French chocolate.

'What a particularly stupid thing to do,' remarked Louisa. 'Who could have imagined that such a crude fraud as that would remain undiscovered? Why not make use of a real grain of wheat?'

'People are very odd,' said her brother.

'Very,' Onslow agreed.

'Now who is this man waving a Bible above his head?' said Louisa, referring to a person in the audience who had leapt from his seat.

'I happen to be able to tell you. That is Admiral Fitzroy,' Dr Powell replied. 'He was captain of the ship in which Mr Darwin sailed to South America, years ago. I confess, I pity Mr Darwin for having been the companion of such a man. I had the misfortune of meeting him the other day.'

Admiral Fitzroy was begging the audience to reject presumptuous human reason. He cried:

'The Book! I call on you to reject with abhorrence an attempt to substitute human conjecture and human institutions for the explicit revelation which the Almighty has himself made in that Book!'

When he had calmed down a little, the last speaker rose on the platform – it was Sir Joseph Hooker, who replied not to the Admiral but to the bishop, thinking that Mr Huxley had not gone far enough. His was a devastating attack, if less pertinent than Mr Huxley's. The bishop, though he was accused by Sir Joseph both of never having read *The Origin of Species* and of being ignorant of the merest rudiments of botany, made no reply. He allowed himself to be attacked. Onslow, as the meeting closed, felt that Wilberforce had failed him.

The speakers came down from the platform and walked out of the hall. Onslow and Anstey-Ward both noticed that the members of the Darwinian party were treated very coldly by the crowd, and Onslow tried to take comfort from the fact that the Darwinians were not being granted a victory, that there were many present loyal to religion and common sense. Yet he could not stop thinking that this was Anstey-Ward's second hour of triumph. Anstey-Ward, however, was less certain of this. He knew that not all those scientists who mattered had been converted to the Darwinian view, even though a great battle of wits had been won.

He glanced across at Onslow. Their eyes met for the second time that day. Anstey-Ward rose from his chair, raised his hat, and smiled. It did not occur to him that this farewell would make his opponent think he was gloating. He had wanted to indicate that theirs was, for the moment, in fact a drawn battle, for he felt pity for Onslow.

28

Three years had passed since the meeting in Oxford. It was the morning of 6th November, 1863, and at Hinterton the Onslows were eating their breakfast.

They ate in silence. Onslow did not regale Louisa with a description of his post, for he assumed that nothing in it would interest her as letters from boys' parents used to do. He received few letters now in any case: Primrose was his only regular correspondent, for most of his other friends had gradually dropped away over the course of years. To them, Onslow in Derbyshire was an admirable but not an interesting figure. Yet their neglect of him was not entirely blameworthy. Onslow was too proud to thrust himself upon those who might not wish to see him now that he was no longer a person of importance, and so he did not attempt to keep in touch with his old acquaintances. They, in their turn, thought he wished to have nothing to do with them in his new, unworldly life – but it did not occur to Onslow that this might be so.

Now, as Louisa finished her muffin, Onslow reached for the second and last of that morning's letters. It was addressed in a hand he did not know, and he thought it must be a bill. Then he turned it over and recognised, unbelieving, the seal of the Prime Minister. Quickly he slit open the envelope, and read:

'*My dear sir, I have much pleasure in informing you that I have received the Queen's command to offer you the See of Ipswich, which has become vacant owing to the demise of the late Bishop. This offer is subject to the condition that the Estates of the See shall be placed under the management of the Ecclesiastical Commission. If as I hope you should be willing to accept the offer, you will perhaps have the goodness to inform me of it without delay. I am, my dear Sir, yours faithfully, Palmerston.'*

Onslow's hands trembled a little as he read, just as they had done when he first received Anstey-Ward's letter. He opened his mouth to blurt something out to Louisa, but then, quite suddenly, he decided not to say anything yet. He re-read the letter and saw that it was true, then quietly folded it and sat thinking. Louisa poured him more coffee, and he said 'Thank you' quite naturally. He gazed out at the grey world beyond the window, and felt warm inside, as though he had in some way triumphed.

It was so good simply to be remembered. Nearly four years had passed since he was last offered anything deeply desirable, and he had begun to fear that he was yesterday's man: for though naturally it pained him to be offered what he could not take, he needed to be thought still worthy of temptation. Onslow wondered whether such an offer would ever be repeated, whether this was the last time. Lord Palmerston had met him and liked him and remembered him. When Palmerston was dead, there would be no one to offer splendid preferments. But perhaps not. Perhaps he would always be at least a reserve candidate in the minds of politicians: Dr Onslow, celebrated Headmaster of Charton, celebrated even after years in obscurity. Some of those politicians would be his ex-pupils.

Onslow took up his letter and left the room. He wanted to treasure the offer in his study, out of Louisa's sight. Briefly, he wondered why her knowing would spoil the pleasure. Perhaps it was because the proffered see was that of Ipswich, Ipswich where she had always hoped to live with him in the palace of her childhood. Louisa might well feel bitter at the fact that at last, too late, Ipswich had been offered to him.

It was odd, thought Onslow in his study, that he did not feel bitter himself. For he had reason to feel so, as had Louisa. He ought not to feel something akin to delight, not when it was impossible for him to accept.

181

Onslow sprang out of his chair and strode over to the mantelpiece. There he saw his reflection in the glass which hung above the fireplace, and he paused to study his forty-seven year old face. It had not changed greatly in the last four years. His hair was still moderately thick, and had not turned grey. There were a couple of light lines in his forehead, and the indentations running down from his nostrils to the corners of his mouth were a little deeper than they had been, but that was all. Louisa had aged far more than he had done. At times she looked almost like a little old woman, but he, Onslow, looked youthful enough still to be reckoned a young man to hold a bishopric.

And he would hold a bishopric. He would accept.

It was as though his heart, his whole body, had expanded to fill the room. The discovery of his own intention excited him so much that he wanted to cry out and run. Pacing the floor, he was sure that Anstey-Ward would do nothing, not after all these years. He was suddenly convinced that Anstey-Ward had not meant what he said, convinced that he had made his demand that he accept no high preferment in the mere heat of the moment. He would let the matter rest when it was announced that Dr Onslow was to be the new bishop of Ipswich, for his anger would be quite cool by now. And then, there was a very important consideration. If Anstey-Ward were to make a scandal after more than three years had passed, he would show himself in a bad light. People would wonder why he had not spoken at the time. And in any case, his threat to make a public scandal had been bluff, mere bluff – Onslow wondered why he had not seen this before.

Anstey-Ward was not an unkindly man, thought Onslow for the first time. Only three months ago he had met Primrose in London, and had asked in the pleasantest way, so Primrose said, after the health of Louisa. He had liked Louisa. He would not wish to disgrace her, to drag her down. For her sake at least, even if for no other reason, he would not object. Onslow had never been so sure of anything in his life.

Then he felt a qualm. He remembered how Anstey-

Ward had smiled at him at that meeting in Oxford, smiled in triumph the last time he saw him. But that, Onslow thought, was over three years ago. Besides, Anstey-Ward was probably so well satisfied by the excellent headway Mr Darwin's views were making in the scientific world and in the popular mind that he would be the more inclined to allow Onslow, the loser, a little compensation.

Onslow sat down at his desk and wrote a letter of acceptance to Lord Palmerston. Then he had the gig brought round and drove himself into Ashbourne, where he posted it. Only once the letter was gone did he begin to grow calmer, and to think of his wife and what she would say. She would surely be delighted to learn that her husband was to occupy her beloved father's see – but it was possible, Onslow realised on his way back to Hinterton, that she would not think he was to occupy it. Telling her, in fact, would be difficult.

━━

'My dear,' said Onslow that evening after dinner, when Louisa was occupied with some Berlin wool-work, 'I have something to tell you.'

'Yes?' she said, looking up.

He came to sit beside her on the sofa, and put a hand on her knee, which surprised her very much.

'You may be much astonished. This morning I received a letter from the Prime Minister, offering me Ipswich. Of course you knew that the see had fallen vacant?'

Louisa, who had refrained from commenting on the death of the old man she had wished to die for years, said:

'It was offered to you?' She felt a pang of mingled anger and regret as she thought of this: no such pleasure as Onslow had experienced.

'Yes, it was offered to me. And I have accepted it.'

There was a long pause; then Louisa said:

'Accepted it?'

'Are you not pleased? Is this not what you have always longed for?'

183

'Are you mad, George? Have you forgotten?' Louisa pushed her work aside. 'I cannot believe it!'

He said: 'No, I have not forgotten. But I believe I am in no danger. After this length of time Dr Anstey-Ward – '

'After this length of time! He said that you should *never* accept any high preferment – length of time has nothing to do with it.'

'I tell you I am certain that he could not have meant it. He made his demand merely in anger. I am very sure he will wish to be involved in no scandal.'

'You did this without once consulting me. You have exposed us to terrible danger without saying one word. I shall never forgive you, George, never.'

'Louisa, do you not wish me to explain why I have done it?'

She got to her feet. 'Explain! What explanation can you give? I tell you George, if you are forced to live abroad I shall not go with you. I shall go to live with Martin and Mamma.'

'Please listen to me.' He had not seen Louisa so angry for years, not since they quarrelled in the train coming back from Poplar House. He did not know what to do – it was worse for him now than it had been then, for now he depended upon her.

She made no reply, but stood staring down at the fire, breathing heavily and clenching her fists. Eventually she said:

'Did you hear what I said?'

'Yes,' said Onslow, 'I heard. I apologise for not having consulted you, that was ill done of me. But you must listen to me, Louisa – you must learn why I think there will be no question of our being forced to live abroad.'

'Very well,' she said coldly. 'Explain if you can, not that I will believe you.'

He began: 'My dear, Dr Anstey-Ward will not be able to stomach being involved in a scandal. He will be forced to let the matter rest. Only think. If he were to expose me, he would expose himself as a species of blackmailer. Remember that he has kept silence for years upon conditions. If he

184

were to reveal all he knows, there would be much wondering at his not having done so immediately. He could not present himself as an upholder of morality – he might have been able to do so had he spoken at the time. And then, do you suppose he will care to have his son's name bandied about?'

'It is not as though his son had done anything wrong. I doubt very much that Dr Anstey-Ward would have scruples about everyone's pointing a finger at Arthur Bright.'

Onslow winced at her naming that name.

'But do you understand what I said? Do you see that I have very little cause to fear he will hold by his word? Louisa, my dear, can you not see that there is hope – a great deal of hope, even if you demand certainty, which I own we cannot have?'

She said nothing, because for all her fear and anger, she was beginning to see that there was hope, agonising hope. Onslow had not made a wild claim that Anstey-Ward must have forgiven him by now: he had produced a cynical reason for the man's keeping silence, and Louisa trusted cynical reasoning.

'Dear, come and sit beside me again.'

After a moment's hesitation she did so.

'If you had only consulted me!' she said, sitting down.

He was delighted by this progress, and said:

'I am sorry for that. I have said so, and do not object to saying it again. But Louisa, I did it largely for your sake. I know how long you have wished me to occupy that see above all others, and I was so much excited – I did not think.'

'Knowing that I would wish it is scarcely a reason for not consulting me,' she snapped. 'Indeed, if you thought you were acting for my sake, you ought above all to have asked my opinion. And I hope that if the worst comes to the worst, you will not turn round and blame me.'

'No, certainly not.'

His submissiveness pacified her. She said:

'George, you have explained matters very glibly, but I am sure that Dr Anstey-Ward is a man who will stop at

185

nothing. I cannot believe it will be as you say, and the alternative is so terrible!'

'At nothing, perhaps, except the desire to show himself in a virtuous light. Dr Anstey-Ward, my dear, is an eminently respectable man – or has the desire to appear so.' Even as he spoke, Onslow suffered a moment's doubt, remembering that Anstey-Ward was an atheist. Louisa did not know that, for he had never told her. But atheists seemed to have changed their nature. Few of them were revolutionaries, as Shelley had been, and Tom Paine. They desired to be thought of as respectable.

There was a long pause, then Louisa sighed:

'Hope is so painful. Far worse in its way than the certainty of disaster.'

'Then you have a little hope, at least?'

She ignored this, and replied: 'But if anything goes amiss, George, remember what I said. I will not go with you.'

'No, my dear,' said Onslow, once more putting a hand on her knee. He knew that there would be no question of his going anywhere other than Ipswich, and so did not remind her that it would be her duty to go with him.

'I am afraid,' said Louisa.

Then Onslow put his arm round her waist, something he had not done for years, and thought with satisfaction that they were truly husband and wife.

29

On November 24th, Anstey-Ward returned to Poplar House after having spent three weeks in Wales on a fossil-hunting expedition. He was greeted warmly by his sister, and after supper, she began to tell him what had happened in the world since he went off on his trip. She knew that he would not have seen a newspaper while he was away.

'Now, there was something else I was so sure would interest you – what was it? Oh yes! Dr Onslow is to be the new bishop of Ipswich. It was announced in all the public prints a fortnight or so ago.'

'Dr Onslow?' said Anstey-Ward.

'Do you not remember him? Christian's old headmaster. He and Mrs Onslow once spent the night here. They came on some errand or other, I have forgotten what it was – I remember thinking it strange at the time.'

'Yes, I remember him,' was all Anstey-Ward said.

'It is a little odd that he has not been made a bishop before this, don't you think? I believe he has spent the last few years quite out of the world – but perhaps he wanted a little rest from responsibility,' said Chatty. She went on: 'I saw Mrs Eames today, and she told me she fears he is rather too High. A great pity. Two High Churchmen on the bench of bishops are more than enough, we were agreed about that. Do you think he will approve of sisterhoods, and confession, like the Bishop of Oxford? I never heard so before – Mrs Eames does tend to exaggerate a little. I wonder where she had her information from.'

'I haven't a notion, Chatty.'

'To be sure, such matters are of no interest to you, more's the pity.'

'You're very right,' said Anstey-Ward, who had never been more fascinated by any piece of information in his life. 'If you and Rose will excuse me, there are matters I must attend to.'

'When you have only just returned?'

'Yes, I fear so.'

His sister watched him go towards the door with indignation in her eyes, but his daughter Rose regarded him speculatively.

In the library, Anstey-Ward sat down in his armchair and pressed his hands to his forehead, as though to force his thoughts into shape. His thoughts were a muddle of incredulity, anger and fear. He was incredulous because he could not believe that Onslow had simply forgotten what he said, though it was a long time ago. He was angry because if Onslow did remember, he was defying him, daring to challenge him – an idea almost as incredible as that of his having forgotten. And he was frightened because he did not know what to do.

At length, after pouring himself some brandy, he decided that he had three choices: to do nothing, to expose Onslow immediately, and to threaten exposure if he did not resign, just as he had done four years before. At first, Anstey-Ward's hatred of having the whole sordid business dug up again made him think that to do nothing was the least unpleasant alternative. Let everything be buried and forgotten – yet the thought of that soon made him sweat with furious anxiety. He pictured Bishop Onslow sneering at him delicately to Canon Primrose, mocking his mere bluster and his lack of resolution, observing that those dogs who barked loudly often had no bite. They might meet one day, and then Onslow would smile at him – an intolerable thought.

But the thought of exposing Onslow to the Prime Minister and the public prints was quite as unbearable. For exactly as Onslow had guessed he would, Anstey-Ward knew that after this length of time he would be showing

188

himself in a very unpleasant light if he were to come forward with the evidence against his enemy, evidence which had been yellowing for years at the back of one of the drawers in his library. People would condemn him either for not having done his duty at the time, or, possibly, for having sat in judgement on Onslow in the first place. No one would think he had acted rightly, and Anstey-Ward wanted to be thought of as a righteous man, just as he could not bear to be thought irresolute. He had blackmailed in the interest of justice and virtue, not merely because he did not wish to involve his son in a scandal – but it was blackmail just the same. He had not thought of that before, and he hated having to realise it.

Savagely he wished that he had destroyed Onslow completely when he had the opportunity, in spite of Onslow's innocent wife, in spite even of Christian. But it was no use, the opportunity was past. There remained only the third choice: to threaten, and hope his threat was heeded. For if Onslow called his bluff, and refused to resign, he would not be able to expose him. He would not be able to face what would follow – the gossip, the outrage, the criticism, the wondering. And if he did not expose Onslow after warning he would do so, the man would be able to laugh at him, able to sneer more heartily even than he would do if no threat were made and the matter were simply allowed to rest. For Anstey-Ward knew that in the second case he might be able to pass himself off as a mere hot-tempered man, content to let bygones be bygones once his anger had cooled. He could not do that if he threatened Onslow again.

Back Anstey-Ward went to thinking that it would be best to do nothing, and then he wavered once more. In the end, caught between two repulsive alternatives, he decided to spin a coin. Heads represented doing nothing at all, and tails represented issuing a threat which he could only hope Onslow would obey out of fear. And Onslow had already shown himself to be recklessly bold.

====

189

At Hinterton, Onslow and Louisa were receiving the congratulations of Mr and Mrs Butterick, who had been in London when it was first announced that Onslow was to be Bishop of Ipswich. Two weeks had passed since then, two weeks in which the Onslows had received the congratulations of all manner of people.

'My dear sir, I cannot tell you how delighted I am that you have accepted the appointment. You have been wasting your talents here, but how we shall miss you!' said Mr Butterick.

'Yes, we shall,' put in his wife, who did not like Onslow, in spite of the fact that he was High Church enough to wear a surplice in the pulpit, something of which she approved. She thought him both cold and arrogant, but she had always been polite to him. 'And we shall miss Mrs Onslow too – her Sunday school.'

'And I am sure we shall miss everyone at Hinterton,' said Onslow. 'We have spent four very happy years here, have we not, Louisa?'

'Oh, we have.' said Louisa. Now that they were to escape from Hinterton, it did seem as though the period they had spent there had not been so very bad.

'Yours is the first admirable appointment to the bench of bishops Lord Palmerston has made,' said Mr Butterick. 'I have never been able to understand his passion for appointing men whose scholarly attainments cannot be said to exist.'

'Oh, that can be put down to Lord Shaftesbury's account,' said Onslow, as he remembered having once said to Primrose. He was enjoying Mr Butterick's praise – he enjoyed everything now. 'Let them only be Evangelicals and nothing else is of the slightest consequence.'

'Then how glad I am for your sake that Lord Shaftesbury did not dissuade Lord Palmerston from giving you your due. We need bishops who are good scholars.'

'We need Dr Onslow,' said Mrs Butterick in a shy voice, 'but I do not think it is of the first important that a bishop should be a scholar. It is of more moment that he should be able to rule his diocese without, without alienating the

190

affections of his clergy and their parishioners. Do you not think so?'

Mr Butterick looked astonished at his wife's venturing a decided opinion.

'Oh yes,' said Louisa, equally taken aback.

'No one, madam, could disagree with you,' said Onslow, observing the expression on Mr Butterick's face, which amused him.

'Am I then the only one amongst us who values scholarship?' said Mr Butterick good-humouredly. 'I cannot believe it! But Dr Onslow, how well pleased you must be that your appointment has been so generally welcomed – even by those who like to write leading articles critical of all that the Government does.'

'Yes,' said Onslow; and Louisa looked at him, thinking that the whole depth of his pleasure had emerged in that one word, and that the Buttericks would consider it odd.

At that moment, the parlourmaid opened the door, carrying a salver on which there lay an envelope. 'A telegram, sir,' she said to Onslow. He took it, and as he did so, he knew that his three-week-old confidence was no more substantial than a fine spider's web, now ripped away from its corner to dangle as a forlorn and dirty string.

The Buttericks were respectfully silent.

'Would you object,' said Onslow, 'if I read this? – my sister in Italy has been unwell.' Although he guessed what the telegram contained, he wanted to see the words. It was possible, just possible, that a telegram was not from Anstey-Ward, but from some impulsive person who wished to offer felicitations.

'My dear Dr Onslow, pray do not hesitate!'

Onslow ripped open the envelope and read:

RESIGN IMMEDIATELY – ANSTEY-WARD.

'May I see it, George?' said Louisa. Silently he handed it to her.

'Not bad news, I trust?' said Mr Butterick.

'Oh no!' said Louisa, gazing at the words. 'No, indeed! Is it not delightful news, George, what a relief – she is better.'

191

'Yes,' Onslow managed to say.

'I am so glad,' said Mrs Butterick politely. 'What has Mrs Jenkinson been suffering from?'

'Oh,' said Louisa, 'oh, she had the misfortune to contract typhus fever. And she has never been strong.'

'What excellent news, then,' said Mr Butterick.

'Yes, it is. We have been so worried.'

'Most unpleasant to be so troubled in mind at such a moment as this is. Or, to be sure, at any moment.'

'Yes, indeed.'

'But now you may be easy. There will be nothing to spoil the pleasure of your removing to Ipswich!'

'Oh, moving house will scarcely be a pleasure. It never is anything but a trouble,' said Louisa. Her voice shook a little, but she soon regained control. 'I so well remember our move from Charton, and how so many things were lost.'

'I think,' said Mrs Butterick, who could see that Onslow was deeply affected by the good news concerning a sister whom he scarcely ever saw, 'that perhaps Mr Butterick and I ought to take our leave of you.'

Louisa got to her feet.

'How very good it was of you to call.'

'Naturally we came as soon as possible to felicitate you, Mrs Onslow,' said Mr Butterick. He wished to remain and talk about the bishopric, but he could not help noticing the way in which Louisa had jumped at his wife's suggestion.

'So very kind.' Louisa looked at Onslow, angry with him for not helping her make the pretence. He used to have perfect self-control – she remembered how he had played his part when they went to visit Anstey-Ward.

'Yes,' said Onslow. 'Yes, indeed. Pray give my regards to Tom, sir.'

'Certainly I shall.'

At last, the Buttericks left, and Louisa and Onslow were alone in the drawing-room.

30

Louisa's eyes fell; clumsily she went over to the sofa and sat down. Onslow turned to look out of the window.

'So it has happened,' he said at last.

'Yes,' she replied, too exhausted by the effort of deceiving the Buttericks to hate him.

'I was so sure – so certain – I suppose he must have been abroad when the announcement was made.'

'Yes.'

Louisa began quietly to cry: not yet with rage at Onslow, but simply because the gleaming prospect of happiness had been snatched away in a moment. And she wondered at her own incredible folly, wondered how in the world she could have thought this would not happen.

'Louisa, do not cry. It makes it so much worse,' he said, hearing one small sob. 'You are not in general so lachrymose.'

She took no notice. She had been so sure that youth and high spirits would return to her once she was installed at Ipswich, with Paris dresses, and important company, and an income of £5,000 a year. Now she would never feel young again.

Onslow turned round from the window and watched her for a while. He supposed he ought to comfort her, but he could not bring himself to do it. He walked out of the room and left her to weep, and then she hated him with all the energy she had left.

Onslow locked himself in his study and went over to his desk, where a half-finished sermon lay on the blotting pad. He took it up and fingered it, looking at the fire. He did not feel tired out, like Louisa. Now that he had escaped from her sobbing, he felt both calm and capable. The thought of what his life was to be now did not oppress him, for he refused to acknowledge that all hope was quite gone. He still clung to the idea that Anstey-Ward feared to expose himself as a blackmailer, and was in fact eager for the suppression of any scandal – that the telegram, in short, was a bluff.

Onslow could not tolerate the thought of submitting to Anstey-Ward's command. The idea of having the man gloat over him, as though he were a captured, helpless specimen, made him flush fiercely and crumple up the sermon in his hand. Never that, he thought, even if he were to be exposed. There was a certain dignity about exposure; he would hold his head high if he were exposed. He told himself that now he had taken his chance, it was his duty to see it through to the end.

Onslow made himself contemplate the worst. He saw himself alone in exile abroad, existing on the £200 a year which was his sole private income. He saw himself alone with his God, shunned by the world, and the picture did not trouble him, because there was something almost heroic about it – certainly there would be if he did not slide down into the moral swamp where involuntary exiles lived, where there was drinking, and card-sharping, and unclean linen. At that moment such an existence seemed distinctly preferable to his life at Hinterton, which was not so bad in itself, he knew, but which was poisoned because he lived it at Anstey-Ward's insistence. And after thinking for two weeks that it was over, he could not bear to crawl back into it. For two weeks, he had been able to think that very shortly he would never see this dark and uncomfortable study again. It was intolerable to think he might write his sermons in it for the rest of his life – the thought was far worse than it had been before he accepted the bishopric.

But almost as soon as he had persuaded himself that he could and would challenge Anstey-Ward again, and endure a lonely life abroad if necessary, Onslow thought of how if

194

Anstey-Ward took up his challenge, and exposed him, he would be not only reviled, but ridiculed.

He remembered how he had once seen one of the vicious cartoons which had been circulated when the Bishop of Clogher was arrested for sodomy, over forty years before. He had come across it some while after he was made Headmaster of Charton, and had yielded to temptation for the first time. The cartoon had called the Bishop 'The Arse-Bishop' in its caption – the memory made Onslow feel ill. Such rollicking brutality was no longer in fashion, but Onslow knew that indescribably coarse material was still circulated, though perhaps more discreetly than it had been in the twenties. He knew that he would be mocked in just such a fashion by Holywell Street pornographers – and though he thought he could stand hatred and exile, he knew that he could not stand being the subject of pornographic ridicule.

Then he thought of how Louisa had said she would not go with him if he were forced to live abroad, and he tried to imagine life without her.

For the first twelve years of his marriage, he had not needed her. Now the case was altered. He knew that while exile with his wife beside him might be less noble than exile without her, it would be far less uncomfortable. In fact, he thought as he sobered down a little, he would not be able to endure the utter loneliness of life abroad if she did not come with him. And she had said she never would – but it must have been an empty threat, for she had always done her wifely duty, and surely would always do it.

Onslow was faced with two equally ugly choices. Even when he thought of what scandal and exile would really mean, the idea of resigning as he had been ordered to do was as repugnant and shaming as ever. Like Anstey-Ward, he could not decide, and he had to decide quickly.

Then Onslow recalled the existence of God, which he had scarcely touched on in his thoughts till now. Looking out of the window, he saw that there was still a little daylight, and in that daylight he could see the church tower, just across the way. He got up, fetched his hat and greatcoat, and went out. On reaching the church, he pushed open the door, and walked up the aisle to kneel in one of the front pews. The church's cold and silence and mustiness enabled him to concentrate upon his God.

He remained kneeling on his hassock for twenty minutes, until it was almost entirely dark. Then the sexton came in, carrying a lantern, and the noise and light disturbed him. Onslow felt almost ashamed of having been caught in prayer, as though the sexton could guess precisely why he needed to pray. Fortunately, the man did not appear to have noticed him, but even when he and his light were gone, Onslow found it hard to recapture his mood of prayerfulness, and reluctantly he got to his feet. Then he made his way back to the rectory.

Though his prayers had been curtailed, they had been successful. God, Onslow believed, demanded that he should place himself unreservedly in the hands of the wife against whom he had so greatly offended. It would be for her to decide.

=====

Louisa turned on Onslow in a fury when he suggested not resigning, and did not appear to take in the fact that it was her decision that mattered.

'To have accepted that bishopric in the first place was madness, see where it has led us, and now you dare to suggest that you will still not resign! It is your fault that we are in this mess. Your fault entirely, and now whatever you do there will be gossip.'

'I am aware.'

'You think it will be humiliating to resign, but you deserve to be humiliated!'

'Perhaps I do, Louisa. But I still think there is a chance.'

'A chance! You have had it proved to you in the clearest possible way that he will ruin you, and still you say there is a chance! Do you want to be destroyed? Do you want to spend the rest of your life abroad? And don't think I will accompany you.'

196

'No, you told me that before. So it is your view that I must resign?'

She drew breath. 'Yes, George, that is my view, though of course I know it will not weigh with you. So be it. I shall write to Martin, telling him to expect me.'

'On the contrary, I am, as I told you, concerned only to please you. If you wish it, I shall resign.'

'Good. And I only hope that you are properly sensible of your own folly.'

'I am. And once again, I ask you to forgive my original fault. Is that in your mind, Louisa?'

She said nothing. She did not like the fact that Onslow, instead of reaching the only sensible decision on his own, had made her do it for him – and therefore she witheld forgiveness. Onslow looked reproachfully at her sullen face, inclined his head as though she were a stranger, and left the room.

Back in his study, Onslow first composed a telegram to Anstey-Ward, to be sent in the morning. It said merely 'I resign – Onslow.' Then he turned his attention to the letter of resignation, which took him hours to write, hours interrupted by a silent dinner with Louisa. At last, the final draft ran:

My Lord,

Three weeks since, your lordship did me the honour of offering the bishopric of Ipswich for my acceptance. I accepted it, but I did so against the dictates of my conscience.

I will not presume to trouble your lordship with details of the nature of my scruples, but will venture to say only that I am much afraid of a worldly ambition which I know to present a grave danger to my soul. I have until so lately, as your lordship may be aware, controlled this perilous ambition, and I therefore refused the various preferments which your lordship was good enough to offer me upon my resigning the Headmastership of Charton School. My resolution to accept neither bishopric nor deanery wavered only when I was offered the see of

197

Ipswich, the reason being that the bishop's palace there has the tenderest of associations for me, for it was there I courted Mrs Onslow.

Yet after many days of thought and prayer, I am writing to your lordship to say that it is my duty to resign the preferment, for I cannot, conscientiously, become a bishop. I do so trusting sincerely that by resigning so shortly after my acceptance, I am causing your lordship no grave inconvenience. Indeed I cannot believe I am doing so, for there are so many men in the Church of England better by far in every way than one who begs leave to sign himself,

Ever your lordship's most obedient servant,
G. R. Onslow.

Hinterton Rectory, November 27th, 1863.